The Coach's Forbidden Temptation

Copyright

Opening Quote

Learning to live this life, coping with the thought of losing you. But my hoping and my praying is no use because the end-all was the be-all, and the last call made me fall harder and farther, and I keep asking why.

Too Far Gone by Ryan Jesse

Chapter One

☪ Hunter ☪

(Two Years Ago)

"I think with that, the team is yours," Able Mason says to me. He's officially retired as Head Coach and is handing off the reins of Brystone Springs University's football team to me. "I'm glad you got the job. This team has the potential to go all the way. Especially with Brystone Springs' All-Stars back together again."

I chuckle. Coach Mason has talked a lot about the five boys from Brystone Springs High School. He really didn't need to, though. I've heard of them myself.

Xavier Remington. Quarterback extraordinaire.

Brant Remington. The best running back Texas has seen in a very long time.

Drake Remington. One hell of a wide receiver. He's got the most yards of any high school player in the entire state.

Kody Remington is one of the best tight ends in the state.

Sterling Remington is another tight end, and I'm excited to see what he can do. He's already got eyes on him from the NFL. I know that because I saw a recruiter for Tampa Bay scouting him at today's practice .

I've had the opportunity to meet most of the team, including all of the All-Stars, but not Kody. I was told he was on vacation with his family. That would be fair. The issue, though, is it seemed like more than a few people knew that wasn't true. I intend to get to the bottom of it.

"I'm lookin' forward to gettin' started, Coach Mason." I reach out to shake his hand. His grasp is firm, even though he's long past retirement age. "I appreciate the rundown and all your help over the week while I settle."

"Be sure you head to the club tonight. You've been through a lot of transition. You deserve the break. Even though you'll technically be working."

I laugh because he's not wrong. I do need a break, but I will be working. Technically. Signing autographs and taking selfies. I played for fifteen years up in Chicago. Football is in my DNA. Playing is my life.

Well, it was. Was my life. I suffered a career ending knee injury just before the playoffs last year. The Guardians still went on to win that Super Bowl, but I was sidelined. When I got through rehab, I got the news. I wasn't going back. I couldn't. My knee isn't strong enough anymore, and I'll forever be walking with a hardly noticeable limp.

I'm thirty-seven-years-old, but I had a couple good years left. My contract still had a year on it. I wasn't ready to hang up my jersey. I was one of the best wide receivers in the league. I was right up there with the likes of Chris Carter and Randy Moss. I loved the game as much as it loved me.

Instead of finishing my career out on a high, though, I was forced into retirement. My agent is the one who pushed me to apply for this job. The second it hit the news that I was retiring, top universities around the country were begging me to coach. I've never wanted to coach, though.

So, why the fuck did I accept this? The simple answer is because after my agent told me about it, I couldn't stop thinking of Brystone Springs. I grew up here. I went to Brystone Springs University. I graduated right from here with several records that have yet to be beat.

But it wasn't just that. This university has been struggling for a few years to get a strong foothold in the muddy field that is college football. Under Coach Mason, Brystone Springs has seen numerous championships. He's been around a while. Hell, he was my coach when I went here. He's one of the best. No question.

It's just that as he's aged, his game has aged as well. His plays are dated, and opposing teams easily run through his team. Even still, Coach Mason instilled several things in my head and heart, including my love for the gridiron.

The issue for both of us is neither of us can let it go. He should've let it go years ago. I should let it go now. I should be a game commentator for ESPN. I got offered that. I was also offered jobs by Fox and all of the other major networks.

I turned them all down for this opportunity; this call I felt to come here. A call I still don't understand. I never wanted to come back here when I left. Once I became a Guardian, I never looked back. For holidays, I flew my parents to me in Chicago. Brystone Springs was as dead to me as the Texas heat is scorching. I never missed it. Never thought of it.

Not until my agent brought it up and told me the school needed a new coach. There was a pull to come back here. Suddenly, all I wanted was home.

My home.

I guess we can take the boy out of Texas, but we can't take Texas out of the man. Or however that saying goes.

I've been back here for exactly one week, and the accent I worked so hard to lose is back full force. Instead of my usual dress pants and nice dress shirt or button down, I'm back in worn jeans and t-shirts. My thin, black, leather belts have been replaced with the thicker ones with larger belt buckles. Dress shoes are out. Sneakers are the only things I wear, but I have a nice pair of cowboy boots for special occasions.

I even replaced my brand new, electric powered Mustang for a sleek, black Ford F150 with all the bells and whistles. I'm in love with my Raptor. It feels so natural being behind the wheel. Anything else I've ever driven simply doesn't compare, and I've been behind the wheel of a lot of fancy cars in my years.

"I guess it's time to get you back to that cozy penthouse you bought, huh?" Coach Mason says.

I bark out a laugh. "I don' know how cozy it is. Pretty empty right now." I rub my stubbled chin before running a hand through my dark brown hair. "Waitin' on furniture."

"Still ain't shown up yet?"

"Nah. Said they'll have it soon, though. Least I got a bed."

"All ya need." Coach Mason slaps me on the back as we walk off the field. "Oh. One more thing." He pulls the lanyard hanging around his neck over his head and hands it to me. "Keys to the kingdom."

I grin my trademark lopsided smirk. "Never thought I'd be the one holdin' these. You were always careful not to let me near them when I played for ya."

It's Coach Mason's turn to laugh as I take the keys. "You were an asshole when you were a kid."

"Still am."

We both laugh as we head back to the locker rooms where my new office is. After saying goodbye to Coach Mason, I unlock the office door and stand in the doorway grinning from ear to ear. After a few moments of taking it all in, I walk slowly into the room.

The desk and chairs need a lot of help. The entire office does, but I'm giddy that it's mine. Coach left me his playbook, and it's centered on the old wooden desk. I sit down in the worn and ripped leather chair and run a finger along the notebook. Red because that's his favorite color.

I open the cover and get lost in all of the old plays, some that I still love using to this day. With my own twist, of course. I wonder if he's watched me play; if he can pick out plays I've run that were inspired by him.

After a while, I glance at my watch and jerk.

Shit. I got fucking lost, I think to myself. I'm supposed to be at Black in less than an hour, and I still need to get home to change. I'm going to relax, but also reintroduce myself to this town as the university's new football coach, but if I get to sign a few autographs along the way, I'm okay with that.

I lock the office door on my way out and hurry to my truck. Brystone Springs is a small Texas town, so it doesn't take me long to reach my building. After parking in the private parking ramp, I quickly make my way to the top floor. It's only accessible to residents, and I love that sense of security.

After parking, I jog to the door and let myself in. No one else lives on my floor, so this entrance is all mine. I control the guests who enter. They can only get in with a code and identification.

I quickly change into a more classy, but still casual, outfit. Jeans with a black button down seems like a good plan. I put cowboy boots on to complete the outfit and run my fingers through my hair, tossling it to give me a messy, but not too unkempt look. It's perfect and drives people wild. I should know. I've had my share of partners over the years. They don't last because they're just not what I want.

The second I arrive at Black, an exclusive club in Brystone Springs, I can see I've underestimated the pull I have. There's a line that wraps around the building, and as soon as someone spots me stepping out of my truck, I'm swarmed with people waving pictures of me and magazines with me on the cover in my face all requesting an autograph.

Like a goddamn angel, a plain clothed cop appears at my side and propels me through the crowd. Security meets us halfway, and I breathe a huge sigh of relief when I'm behind the closed and locked door of the club.

"Holy fuck," I rumble.

"There's a lot of people and media out there," the cop says to me. "I'm Colton. Colt for short. I work with Brystone Springs Police Department. We have several bouncers here tonight that work for the club, but I also have some other guys in uniform coming to help with crowd control."

"I thought this was an RSVP event," I say, a little dumbfounded. "How many people are out there?"

"Hundreds. And the club is at max capacity tonight with people who did RSVP. So, a lot of those people are just from around the town and surrounding area."

I rub my head. "Jesus. I didn't count on that. I'm gonna have to hire security. Don't need them camping outside my building."

"Might be a good idea, Mr. Steele," Colt says to me.

"You can call me Hunter."

Colt smiles. "Appreciate it." He gestures ahead of him. "There are a lot of people here already. I'm sure they'd love to see you make an entrance. VIP section is just straight through the kitchen here and up the stairs."

I nod and follow a bouncer. We stop so I can wave to everyone before I'm ushered up the stairs and to my table in the VIP section. I notice there's a couple of groups already there. One of the groups is some of my players, including the All-Stars, sans Kody.

I narrow my eyes slightly because I still think there's something fishy going on with them. We had our first practice today before I had that final conversation with Coach Mason. Everyone said goodbye to the beloved coach, who promised to cheer them on from the stands every

8

game, but Kody still wasn't there. Missing practice without letting me know personally is punishable and is a rule I implemented today because of this situation.

"Hey, y'all," I say when I reach the table of my team.

"Hey, Coach Steele. Good practice today, huh? I think you'll fit right in," Xavier says. He's a good leader. I can already see his skills. There's a reason he and his cousins are All-Stars. They're all incredibly talented and leaders in their own right.

"Yeah, it was. Don't really like that we had someone missing from practice today, though. I don' know Coach Mason's rule, but mine's no one misses practices without me knowin' or they can be benched for the season."

Drake winces as he looks up at me. "He's -"

Sterling cuts him off, and my eyes flick to his just as hard ones. "He's with his family. Shit happened, and they got delayed. He won't miss another one."

I nod. "He better not. Enjoy the night, y'all. See ya tomorrow." I turn and head for my table. I'm by myself tonight, and that's by design. Usually, I'd have some random girl on my arm, but that's not how I'm working tonight. New job, new life, new habits.

I'm tired of hiding who I am.

After a couple hours of a steady stream of controlled chaos, I signal for a break. I've signed many autographs, taken several selfies, given out way too many hugs, and I'm fucking tired.

"What can we get you, Mr. Steele?" the club's owner asks me, appearing at my side. Nice guy. Short. He's a good six inches shorter than my six-feet-five-inches, but he makes up for the height difference with attitude and humor.

"I need to get somethin' to eat and stretch my legs. A good drink would be nice."

"I'll have the kitchen make something for you now. If you'd like, you can follow me down there and hang out back there. No one will bother you there. Bathrooms are right across the hall from the kitchen. I'll grab you a drink."

I nod and follow him, a bouncer sticking close. I order their best bourbon and hide out in the kitchen while they make me some chicken wings. Once I wolf the wings down, and down three drinks, I head for the bathroom before getting back to my duties. I feel a lot more relaxed and confident I can balance my fame and quiet life, at least that's what I hope I get here. Quiet.

Boundaries. It's all about boundaries.

The hallway isn't that well lit, and with the alcohol coursing through my veins, I stumble.

"Woah. You good?" a deep, masculine, velvety voice says from behind me as strong arms and a solid body steady me.

My heart does a somersault as my stomach involuntarily clenches. My breath catches in my chest, and my dick immediately hardens. Thank all the Gods that it's fairly dark because I'm very well-endowed. A boner is extremely difficult to hide.

I clear my throat and turn as the man releases me slowly, making sure I'm good to stand on my own two feet. "Yeah. Yeah, I'm good. Drank a bit too much, too fast."

"Happens to the best of us."

I hear the words somehow, but the roaring in my ears is loud. I'm drowning fast in this man's golden hazel eyes. He's just a couple inches shorter than me and obviously works out. He's in incredible shape. I'd place him in his twenties.

I don't know if it's just me, but I feel like our lips are getting closer. Like some magnetic force is pulling us together. I'm completely powerless to stop it, and I don't want to.

I don't want to hide anymore.

I'm gay. Girls have always been just a front. I've never fucked any of them. My sexual satisfaction came from a very secret, very exclusive club. Every person I was ever with signed an NDA, non-disclosure agreement. My secret has been kept for years, but something about this man makes me want to throw caution to the Texas wind.

When our lips touch, electricity zips through me. My cock is dangerously close to ripping through my jeans. I reach up and grab him around the back of the neck. I angle his head so I can thrust my tongue into his mouth and take control of this kiss.

He has my world spinning. His taste makes me feral. I growl when he groans.

I never want this to end.

Chapter Two

☪ Kody ☪

The tall drink of water pushes me against the wall near the bathroom door after I drag him into it to continue our hot kiss we started in the hallway. I have a reputation to protect. I'm a ladies' man. My dick has been wet inside numerous different ones.

No one needs to know that in order to get hard and finish the job, I need to envision a hot guy. Someone like Ryan Reynolds or Hugh Jackman. Travis Kelce never fails me. The girl always leaves happy.

And I leave feeling empty inside, but it doesn't matter to me. All that matters is my true self isn't shown to anyone, not even Drake, my cousin who is more like my brother. None of my cousins can know. Not my family. Friends. Teammates. No one.

It's not that I'm homophobic or anything. Two of my cousins are gay and happily in relationships with the loves of their lives. Xavier has a good life with Colton. He already married him, and he's just going into his Sophomore year of college. Drake has just as an incredible one with his boyfriend, Blade.

The problem is that I hear how people talk. Texas is weird. Maybe people have no issue with the LGBTQ community, but some… Well, some aren't okay with it. It's probably like that in the rest of the world, but the difference is that in Texas, everyone carries a gun. Never know if showing

11

affection for a man will get me shot. I'd go to war for my cousins and their sexuality being defended, but being shot... it's a real fear for me.

I don't care right now. My heart is racing. The pull to him is so strong. Too strong. Everything inside me is screaming for him to ruin me. I need him to after everything that's happened to me in the last week.

So as he dominates the kiss, I sink into him and cling to him for dear life. Each stroke of his tongue against mine drowns out memories of what my last female conquest threatened to do to me. It's been a lot harder and harder for me to focus enough to get it up. I couldn't do it for her, and after she screamed and cried for hours about how she must be ugly, she switched it up to how she's going to expose me because I have to be gay if I can't get it up for her.

It's the truth, but there's no fucking way anyone will believe her. I've laid too much of a foundation with my rep for one person to ruin it.

The issue is I'm starting college now. If I'm struggling with high school girls, how the hell am I gonna do with college girls? It's not like I won't have plenty. I'm on the football team, and my reputation already precedes me.

Maybe a secret pounding in the bathroom of Black will give me more time to figure out what the hell I'm gonna do. I can fantasize about this handsome stranger when I need to get off. I know my family and friends won't judge me for being gay. It's everyone else I fear.

"Are we gonna just kiss, or are you gonna fuck me?" I grip the man's ass. He's driving me crazy. He's well built, a few inches taller than my six-feet-two-inches. He's muscular; built like a goddamn truck. I want nothing more than for him to plow me over and over.

Make me forget.

I've been in hiding since the night Cassie, the girl I was with, threatened to expose me. I went into a deep depression. I was so fucking pissed at myself for being like this and damn near jumped off a bridge. Drake saved my life when he pulled me back. I had no idea he'd followed me, but instincts made him believe something was wrong with me.

I still haven't told him what it was. How far into that depression I got.

I haven't told anyone. To his credit, Drake never told my parents. He did tell our cousins, though, and that might be worse. They're all watching me very closely.

"Fuck," the man growls. His teeth catch my lower lip. I groan as he tugs it and sucks. He releases it and roughly turns me around so my chest instead of my back is against the wall.

This bathroom is for one person only. I locked the door the second it closed, and we chose to forego the light. It's better that way. I got enough of a glimpse of him in the hall. He'll be forever burned in my mind. He's the most beautiful and dangerous looking man I've ever laid eyes on. There's nothing I wouldn't let him do to me. I need to be used; feel wanted.

In a hurry, I unbutton my jeans. I feel him doing the same behind me. My ass isn't a virgin. I've had sex with guys before. Just in another state and not as often as I'd like. It's been too long since I've been stretched.

"I can't wait anymore," I groan, bracing myself.

"Yeah ya can."

I hear his saliva as he wets something down. I hope like hell it's his hand and he's stroking his dick, using the wetness as lube before he slams into me. I start stroking my dick at the thought and push back against him.

"Oh, fuck yes." I squeeze my dick as I close my eyes and stroke.

"Did I say you could touch yourself?" He teases my hole with wet fingers before sliding two of them inside me, coaxing them hard and fast as he slaps my ass.

The tone of his voice has me instantly letting my cock go and slapping my other hand against the wall. I grit my teeth to keep from screaming out how good his fingers feel. "No, sir," I answer.

He starts slowly fingering me like it's a goddamn reward for my obedience, and all I want is to keep doing everything he says.

"Good boy. Next time, say daddy."

"Fuck yes." I arch into him and clench around his fingers. I'm ready. So fucking ready.

"Fuck yes, what?" he breathes against my neck before biting it as he thrusts.

I can't stop the grin. This is everything I need. Everything. Dirty sex in a bathroom with a stranger I'll never see again who is helping me live out every fucking fantasy I've ever had. "Fuck yes, daddy."

"That's my boy," he rumbles. "Ready to take daddy's long, thick, cock in that tight little hole of yours?"

"Oh God, yes. Fuck me, daddy. Please."

13

He pulls his fingers out of me slowly, and I already miss them, but he doesn't keep me waiting long. I feel the tip of his dick against my hole along with the unmistakable feeling of a condom. I didn't even hear him remove the wrapper.

"Wait. Latex," I say, briefly coming to my senses.

"Latex free, baby. I'm cautious. Always. I got you." And with no more words, he thrusts his dick deep inside me.

I fall against the wall with a low moan as my eyes roll back in my head. "Fuck," I hiss, my ass squeezing around his cock.

He moves a hand down my body to my still painfully erect length and grips it. He strokes slowly, but doesn't thrust into me, instead allowing me to get used to his size. He's the biggest I've ever taken by far, and for a moment, I regret everything about what's happening right now.

But that's not how this gorgeous creature works. He slowly works me until I relax. He thrusts steadily and gently, opening me up more and more for him. Before I know it, my quiet hisses turn to moans that are getting louder and louder. I'm leaking precum, and he's using it to coat my dick, making his hand slide over me easier.

The sensations of being stroked and fucked at the same time is too much for me. My thighs start to tremble. My cock twitches in his hand and gets even harder. I can feel my orgasm start low in my back. It won't be long before I'm shooting ropes of come against the wall, painting it in my essence.

The man grunts against my neck as he thrusts into me harder and faster. If his hand wasn't protecting me, my cock would be slapping against the wall.

"Fuck, I'm gonna come, daddy. Please let me come," I growl through gritted teeth.

"Not fuckin' yet. Be my good boy. Just a little longer."

It takes every fiber of my being to not come, especially since he's still stroking me. Faster… faster… My nails dig into the wall, and I grip it as hard as I can.

Moments later, I feel his dick spasming inside me. His come fills the condom, and I wish like hell it was me. But it doesn't matter because it still feels warm and like fucking heaven and hell simultaneously.

"Fuck yes, daddy!" I shout, somehow managing to keep my voice low.

He pulls out quickly and turns me around. He pushes me back against the wall as he drops to his knees. "Give daddy that sweet come, my good boy." And with that, his hot mouth is hoovering my cock.

I have no other choice but to grip his short hair and hold on for dear life. It takes him only seconds to finish me off. My head falls back against the wall. I see stars as I shoot my unending load down his throat. My entire body is trembling. I slap one hand over my mouth to keep myself from screaming out in ecstasy.

Ruining it, though, someone jiggles the door handle. The man pops his mouth off my dick, and I groan. "Find another bathroom," he growls, his tone icy.

"Come on, man, I gotta go."

"Walk the fuck away!" he commands. I'm sure the dude on the other side of the door jumps and runs, but his voice sends shivers of lust down my spine.

I thought one night of this would be enough. Get it out of my system so I can keep living my lie.

I was wrong. One time will never be enough.

I sense he stands. I can hear him buckling his jeans again. "That was fun. Thank ya," he drawls.

I can feel myself blush as I bend down and pull my pants up. "Anytime. Like tomorrow and any day after that. Preferably all of them." I grin.

"Appreciate it, but this was a one time thing. Wait five minutes before ya leave." He exists out the door and turns on the light on his way before I have a second to react.

I close my eyes and rub them against the sudden flood of brightness. By the time I've adjusted and pulled the door open to stop him, he's gone.

I look up and down the hall. I even walk to the end of the hall and look for him, but I don't see him in the sea of people. I didn't really see him long enough before our lips were ravishing each other anyway. I probably wouldn't even recognize him if I saw him again.

Who the fuck am I kidding? I'm never getting that man's face or voice out of my head.

☪ ☪ ☪

(Present Day)

I sit up in bed gasping and gripping my chest. I look around my room as the club fades out. As my eyes adjust, the walls of my own bedroom start becoming more clear and focused.

"Dream. That fucking dream again."

I look down and groan when my hard as a rock cock strains painfully against my underwear. I reach down and grip it as I lay back down. The hard on is a constant reminder of the biggest fuck up of my entire life.

Two years ago was one of the hardest times of my life. I was transitioning from high school to college. I didn't realize it would be so hard for me. I had a good life and reputation in high school. Going into college, I was no longer one of the big men on campus anymore. I didn't know what to expect, even though I had my cousins and had been recruited to Brystone Springs University's football team. We were all back together and would be playing again. We'd be navigating it all together.

What I didn't expect was my problem with my sexuality hitting me so damn hard. I was in complete turmoil and having the worst identity crisis anyone has ever seen. The week before we started practice, a new coach was taking over.

Hunter Steele.

I had no idea who the fuck he was. I'd never seen him before. Didn't know a thing about him and didn't want to. What I wanted was to be left alone to try and figure out who the fuck I was. I almost jumped off a bridge and went on a bender that week. I missed the first practice and Coach Mason's goodbye because I was so fucking hung over. Not even my cousins or parents could reach me. Hell, I didn't even know if I wanted to go to college. I didn't know if I wanted to play football.

That night, I was supposed to go with my cousins to the Black Club. Hunter Steele was supposed to be there. I found out he was some great football player who retired because of a knee injury and became our new coach. I really didn't care, but if it meant alcohol, I was there.

I was late, though, because I had a few drinks prior and passed out. I woke up a couple hours after I was supposed to be there. When I did get there, I beelined for the bathroom because I felt sick. I'm sure there was still way too much alcohol in my blood, but I still didn't care. It was better than trying to deal with figuring out who I was.

I met this gorgeous man in the hallway on the way to the bathroom. I wasn't thinking straight, and I don't think he was either. Moments after we locked eyes, our tongues were down each other's throats. Seconds after that, we were in that bathroom fucking.

It was the best sex I've ever had and sobered me up quickly.

It wasn't until the next day I figured out who the stranger who fucked me senseless was. I came face to face with him at practice after my cousins and parents had a fuck of an intervention with me. I worked. I went. And there he was. He was as forbidden as the apple on that stupid tree in the Garden of Eden.

Hunter Steele.

My coach.

Chapter Three

☪ Hunter ☪

"Wrap it up!" I yell after blowing my whistle. It's the teams signal to get off the field for a debrief before they hit the showers. I've been coaching this team for two years now. They all know me pretty well.

A few are high-fiving each other on the way over to me. Kody hangs back, but I can see how proud he is of executing his role in this play perfectly every single time we've done it. He should be proud. That was the best playing I've ever gotten out of him.

Once everyone is huddled around me, I look for Kody. He's standing next to Sterling with his eyes down and helmet in his hand. I'm instantly worried. For two years, he's been nothing but sassy. We've gone head to head numerous times, but always take a giant step back before either of us touch each other again.

The first time was a mistake. One that could cost me my career, but I don't care about that. What I care about is him finishing his college career and getting recruited to his dream team, the Dallas Cowboys. If anyone finds out that I fucked him one night in the bathroom at Black Club, that would be the end for both of us.

Not to say it's not fucking hard to stay away from him. Every time I see him with a girl hanging on his arm, I can barely control the possessive monster inside screaming that he's mine.

And he damn well is.

He's been mine ever since that night, and we both know it. We know it well. Just because we can't do anything about it doesn't mean it's not the truth.

"Good practice, y'all. I'm proud of how these plays were run and the openness to trying new things. I think we've got a real shot at bringin' home another trophy this year. The only thing I need to say is keep moving cohesively. You're a team. One person can't do it all. The second we lose that, is the second we fail. Bearin' that in mind, I expect you all to show up at the bonfire tonight being held at Brant's house. We're a team on and off the field. Anyone who doesn't show up causes the entire team to run laps. Don't do that to your teammates. Anyone who can't show up, come talk to me. Hit the showers!"

Everyone jogs off the field. I start to follow but stop when I see Kody hasn't moved an inch. So, I stay where I am and wait for him to say something. When he looks up at me, though, the sadness in his eyes breaks my heart.

"Aren't you gonna tell me what I'm doing wrong?" he asks softly.

All at once, it hits me. I've been a complete asshole to him in order to keep him at a distance. I've nitpicked every single move he's made. Every time he got mouthy, I made him run laps or do push ups. Over the past two years, not once did I notice that he's been getting more and more quiet. Less and less loud and bold with me.

But he has, and I see it all very clearly now.

"Oh, Kody," I say low, looking around to make sure no one sees what I'm about to do. What I can't resist doing. I step closer to him. Every part of me is on fire for him, just like it always is whenever he's around. I look around again before caressing his arm. "Kody, I -"

"I can't do this, Coach. It's been two years. Every time I'm around you, my heart feels like it's going to explode. I know all the reasons we can't do this, but this sexual tension between us is too much." Kody shakes his head. I feel his arm trembling, and I give it a little squeeze. "I'm quitting the team." He starts to walk away.

I panic and grip his arm tighter. My chest tightens, and I have to use all of my willpower not to shout. "What? No. I'm not allowing that."

"You don't have a choice. I've already decided. I'm telling my cousins then going to the administration Monday." He starts to walk away again, but I spin him towards me instead.

Doing something I'll probably regret, I pull him in my arms and hug him hard. "No. I'm not allowing it. I'll walk away from coaching if it means you stay. I'll find you a better coach. One more capable of holding his feelings back. But I'm not letting you give this up. This is your dream. I'm not standing in the way of that just because I'm fucking in love with you and can't have you the way I want you."

My words cause a sob to burst from Kody's chest, and he grips the back of my shirt like he's holding on for life. Like he's drowning and I'm his life raft. I feel the pain he's barely containing, and it shatters me. Is this how I've been making him feel, or is there more going on right now that I don't know?

"I just can't do this anymore. I want to be able to say -"

"Let's talk tonight," I say on a whim. "I'm not tryin' to be an asshole right now. I just want to have a proper conversation alone. Not in the middle of the stadium. You deserve better than that."

"No, I don't," Kody whispers as he pulls away.

"Yeah, ya do." I wipe away his tears. "Take a shower. I'll see you at Brant's in a few hours."

"Can it be before that? Can we just meet somewhere?"

I think about it for a few moments before sighing and dropping my arms from him, though it's the last thing I want to do. "Come to my house. It's the most private place I can think of. I'll text you the access code and get things set up so you can just drive in. Give me your student ID, and don't tell a fucking soul about this."

"I won't," he says. "My ID is in my gym bag in the locker room."

"Put it on my desk before you go. Give me two hours to set things up. Now, go. Please. If you're near me for another minute, all hell is going to break loose. I've held back for way too long. I don't know if I can anymore after having my arms around you like that."

He gives me a soft smile before jogging off to the locker room. I follow, but walk far enough back to maintain my distance and sense. Anyone who saw me hugging him wouldn't think anything of it. Coaches are often close with their players. We're all a little family out here. We have to be close like that, or we'll never get anywhere. That's why I do team building exercises and events. The closer we are, the better we'll be.

So, I'm not worried about that. What I'm truly worried about is the pain Kody was hiding behind his eyes. He's in absolute agony, like he was injured on the battlefield and is fighting not to bleed out. That's the reason

20

I agreed to let him come to my house to talk instead of doing it at the bonfire tonight. Sure, I can get him alone there to talk, but I don't think he can handle it. Something big is going on. Something I sense I'm the only one who can help him with.

☾ ☾ ☾

Two hours later, I open my door and let Kody into my penthouse. I don't bring people here. The only person who's been here is my best friend and agent, Cal. My penthouse is my sanctity. I don't let anyone ruin it for any reason.

But something tells me I need to let Kody in. Not just to the penthouse, but also my life.

I hand him a Pepsi as he plops on one end of my couch. He takes it, and I have a choice. I can take my Pepsi and sit in a chair. That's what I should do. Keep my distance. I could sit down on the other end of the couch. It allows me to be kinda close, but still keep my distance.

But I'm not at all logical when it comes to him. I sit down on the couch right next to him. I expect a look of shock, but when he doesn't even glance at me, I'm completely on edge.

"Talk to me," I say as I lean back.

"It's not that easy, Coach. I don't even know where to start."

"I'm not Coach here. Call me Hunter. How 'bout from the beginnin'?"

"You don't want me to do that. It's a sad story filled with a lot of heartbreak hidden behind an asshole exterior and maybe a suicide attempt or two after a few drunken nights."

I can barely take in air around the knot he has forming in my throat. "Tell me, Kody. It's not a request."

Kody leans forward and puts his Pepsi on the table after he takes a drink. He puts his elbows on his knees and stares straight ahead into my kitchen. I don't dare make a move. I sense he needs this little bit of space while he talks, and all I want is to know what's happening; why my heart feels like it's constricting in my chest.

"That first night at Black, I didn't know who you were. I knew we had a new coach coming in. I knew who he was and knew his rep, but I didn't care much beyond what I was told. I hadn't really even seen a pic of

21

you anywhere because I didn't care. You didn't play for the Cowboys, so I wasn't interested."

"Thanks," I say teasingly with a small smirk as I focus on him.

I see him smile just slightly, and it eases me a little bit. "The next day when I saw you and figured out who you were, I became obsessed. I needed to know every little thing about you. Stats on and off the field. Everything. And over the past two years, I've spent a lot of time memorizing everything about you that you've let slip. I know you love pecan pie and hate apple. I know you despise pistachios."

It takes all of me not to reach out and touch him. "I've done the same, you know. After I figured out who ya were, I instantly backed off. I pulled you aside. We had our talk about how there can never be anythin' between us. That didn't stop me from findin' out everything about ya that I could, though. I hadn't taken the time to look through the team pics. It would've saved us both if I had. But ya had to have left. I was in VIP. You never came up to be with your cousins."

Kody shakes his head. "No. You wouldn't have seen me. I looked for you and left right away when I didn't see you. I should never have tried to show up there in the first place. I wasn't in the best frame of mind. I'd just come off a suicide attempt and spent the entire week drinking. The next day, after the club, my parents and cousin intervened and sat me down. There was a long talk and a lot of crying."

"Hang on. Suicide attempt?" My heart stops beating altogether. I lean forward and drop a hand on his thigh, unable to hold back.

He still doesn't look at me, but he doesn't pull away. "Yeah. I was having a hard time with my sexuality. No one knew I'm gay. No one knows that now. Well, except you. And by my research, I guess the world doesn't know you are either, but that's not the point. I hid myself from everyone. I fronted a normal guy with a lot of sexual partners because it's what was expected. But going into college, things felt different. I knew it wasn't going to be easy, and I was worried about it. I was with this girl at the time, and I couldn't get it up. It happened a few times, and I just couldn't do it. I couldn't even get hard enough to fake it. It was like the more and more I tried to fuck a girl, it didn't matter how many times I imagined someone else like I usually had done. My tricks didn't work, and she got sick of it. She screamed at me for a while about how I must not think she's pretty. Then, she threatened to tell everyone I'm gay."

"Oh, Kody." I let go of his thigh and put my arm around his waist instead so I can pull him close.

Again, he doesn't resist. It's like he's just so tired that he's given up. Given what he just told me, that's worrisome. I know he's avoiding telling me about the suicide attempt, but I'm not letting it go. Just like I'm not letting him go. Not again.

I feel him take a deep breath before he starts talking again. "I felt like everything was spiraling. I was getting depressed. Everyone could see it, but I kept saying I was fine. Before I could really stop myself, intrusive thoughts won. I was so pissed off at myself for not being brave enough to come out like Drake and X. I'm still afraid. I haven't seen them get a lot of hate, but I feel like I might. And it was the same that night. It was too much. I couldn't come out, but I couldn't keep fucking girls when I fucking hated it so much. And I felt like shit for leading the nice girls on. Making them think there might be something when I knew there never would be was the worst part. I felt like the scum of the Earth. A failure. Completely fucked up beyond repair. I'd been getting a little too drunk the few days before, and that night, I just decided that was it. My cousins were at my house. I went for a drive."

He trembles a little, and I tighten my grip. "I got you, Kody. It's okay."

"I got to the bridge. The intent was to drive off it, but I chickened out. Instead, I pulled over and walked to the edge. Before I lost my nerve, I just started climbing over the guardrail. Drake had followed me. I didn't know that. He pulled me back over just as I was about to jump. I'm sure you know that Brystone Springs Creek runs under that. And that was in the summer. There wasn't anything there to catch me. Not a lot of water to break the fall. I definitely wouldn't have made it."

"Fuck, Kody." I pull him into my arms just as the dam he's been fighting breaks. I press my lips against his neck and hug him tightly against me.

Just like on the field, he wraps his arms around me like I'm his lifeline and grips the back of my shirt, fisting the fabric as he soaks my shirt in his tears. I say nothing. I do nothing but hug him and kiss his neck. It takes him several minutes before he's calm enough to start talking again, but I'm not letting him go. I keep both arms locked around him.

"Drake told my cousins, of course. I begged him not to tell my parents or cousins. He compromised on my parents, but told me if he feels like things aren't improving, he's telling them. The night at Black was my last chance. When I texted them and told them I didn't feel well, they said they'd see me at home. When they got there, I had cried myself to sleep, but I didn't drink. I'd thought about the bridge again, though, and that scared me. After practice the next day, I went home with Drake. My cousins were there. So were my parents. It was the intervention I needed. I didn't even fight it. I went to counseling, worked a lot of shit out, and haven't drank any alcohol since. Not even champagne at any of my cousin's weddings. I haven't had a single bad thought. I was even working out my sexuality. I haven't fucked anyone since you. I was in a pretty good place." He pauses as he turns so he's facing forward again. I hate that he lets go of me, but I'm not releasing him. He's staying where he is.

"Was?" I ask quietly.

He takes a deep breath. "Yeah. Was. I just... Last night, I couldn't sleep. I kept thinking of you and just realized that I can't do this anymore. It hurts too much to be near you knowing I can't have you. I don't want you to lose your job. I don't want you to be rocked in scandal if we were to be caught. You're right. It's best to stay away. I'd rather risk my dreams than sacrifice the life you've built. Everyone in this town loves you. The team adores you. I just make things more difficult. And I'm a complete fuck up anyway. I can never do anything right."

"Jesus, Kody. Is that what ya think? That couldn't be further from the truth."

He chooses that moment to look at me. I expect his eyes to be flashing with anger, but that's not what I get. All I see is deep rooted pain and despair. I know I'm the one who put it there. I nitpicked everything he did and made him feel inadequate when he's one of the best players on the team. He's one of the greatest college tight ends I've ever seen, and he already has the stats to prove that.

"All I got was praise in high school, Hunter. Ever since I hit college, I've sucked. I run more laps than everyone else. I can't run a fucking play right to save my life. It's probably because all I can think of is you. It's why I need to -"

"Stop," I growl dominantly. His eyes flare, and he closes his mouth. I swallow down all of the thoughts of what I want to do with him because that's not what he needs. "I'm sorry, Kody. You ain't a bad player. You're one of the best on that team. I never shoulda said otherwise and made you feel like that, and I'm sorry for that. Deeply. I'm sorry I ever made you feel like you weren't good enough, Kody. I shoulda seen your confidence startin' to wane. I was too wrapped up in keeping us distanced for both of our sakes. I went about it the wrong way. I see that now, but that's no excuse. I shouldn't have done it all."

"So…, you… don't think I'm dragging the team down?"

"Fuck, baby. No. No, I don't. You're an integral part of that team." I don't hesitate to pull him into my lap so he's straddling me as I lean back.

His eyes are wide, and he pushes against my shoulders, but I don't let him. "What are you doing? Hunter, you're right. This can't be. And I can't handle a one time thing again. I'm already too far gone with you."

"Who said this was a one time thing?" I ask. I let my hands roam his back as my voice falls to a far more husky tone while I stare into his gorgeous golden hazel eyes.

"Don't tease me. My heart can't handle it. Last night was hard, Hunter."

"I don't want ya to have days like that ever again. I'm sorry I was the cause of it. I don't wanna let ya go, and I'm not going to."

"What about -"

"I don't care. I don't care about the coachin' job. I don't care about the rep. What I care about is you. We'll figure this out. It'll be on the down low. We need to be careful, but not for me. We need to be careful for you. I don't want you gettin' kicked out."

"I feel like I'm dreaming."

I shake my head. "You're not. This has all gone on long enough. You confessed all of this to me. I think it's time ya hear my story."

Kody hesitantly leans forward, but I bring him the rest of the way. He leans his forehead against mine and closes his eyes as he lets out a breath. "I'd like that," he whispers.

I'm glad he doesn't see my sad smile because I don't think he'll like any of this.

Chapter Four

☪ Kody ☪

"I'm a lot like you. The difference is I don't have support. I'm sure my best friend would be fine with me being gay, but I know my family won't be, and I sure as hell don't think the world will be. At least not when I was a pro football player. I don't know how it would go over now with the public, but they don't really matter to me. It's the family. Friends." Hunter pauses for a moment and takes a deep breath.

I shift so I'm sitting next to him with my legs across his lap. He knows I've been getting cramps in my calves lately. He's made sure the trainers are working with me to help. Without a second of hesitation, he starts rubbing my legs as I let out a breath and lean my head against the back of the couch, closing my eyes.

"My parents threatened to kick me out when I was younger. I tried comin' out to them. They basically said it better be an April Fool's Day joke or they'd kick me out. Cut me off. No more college. No chance at the NFL if I couldn't get a recruiter to look at me. I weighed my options quick. Told them it was an April Fool's Day joke. Haven't told a soul since. All of my partners were from very private clubs. Everyone signed an NDA. My secrets been safe for years, but I'm pretty miserable. I'd even contemplated a marriage of convenience just to keep my cover."

My heart hurts for him, but I get it. "That's what I feel like is going to happen to me. I have a friend I considered confiding in. I don't think she'd tell anyone. I was going to propose a relationship for the public just so I can keep my cover. But I hate the idea of doing that to her."

"You should also hate the idea of doing it to yourself. Keeping this secret as long as I have has caused a lot of damage, too. Not to anyone but myself, but it's there. I'm not happy with myself or the decisions I've made. Would I do it again? Probably. At least up until I met you."

I can't help but chuckle. "Yeah. You would've avoided the bathroom encounter all together."

He smiles a little. "I wouldn't say that." He keeps rubbing my calves. The contact is soothing parts of me I didn't know were cracked.

"You wouldn't have?"

He looks at me. "I don't think you realize how life-changin' that night was for me. I've never felt a connection like that with anyone."

My heart skips a beat, but I still need to know. "Then why did you leave so fast? Last night, I started getting in my head that it was because of me. Like I was that bad or something."

"God, baby, no." He shakes his head and focuses on my legs again. I see the regret, though, before his eyes drop. "I got scared. That was the best sex I'd ever had. Not because it felt good. It felt amazing. But it felt that way because of that instant connection I had to you. It came just after that moment in the hallway. I've never in my life been drawn to someone so fast. I've never fucked anyone in a bar. I've never experienced any of the feelings I experienced that night. Scared the fuck out of me, Kody."

We fall into a tense silence. I want to say something, but I can't. Not just yet. I'm still basking in the fact that he knew exactly what I needed when I put my legs in his lap. The fact that I just naturally trusted him, and he naturally gave me what I needed without asking questions makes my heart happy.

He leans forward and grabs my Pepsi. He hands it to me, and I take a long drink amazed at how he just knew I needed it. "How do we do this, then?" I finally ask. "How do we navigate being together if that's what we both want and need while not ruining both of our lives?"

"Keep it quiet. That's what we do. Keep it quiet until I can figure it out. I've never looked into the school policies because I figured they'd be the same as everywhere else. No faculty student relationships. Same with coach and player. I doubt it would be different, but we still need to figure out our options. If it's against school policy, we need to be very careful. If it's not, then I think we'll still need to be careful. We just need a plan going forward."

"What if we get caught?" I focus on the can in my hand.

"Then we deal with it then. What we need to figure out now is if this is somethin' we want to commit to. Because I think it's gonna be tough until you're graduated. We're two years away from that."

I keep my eyes down and nod. I don't know exactly where that will lead us. I'm nervous. "I need to tell my cousins…" I trail off. "And my parents."

"Do you think they won't support you?"

I shake my head. They'd never do that to me. I take a deep breath. "I know they'll support me. It's not that. It's just that I should've come out a long time ago. I think they'll be disappointed that I kept this from them."

It takes Hunter a few minutes to look back at me. "What if we did it together? What if I called up the people I need to and gave them the news?"

I look at him quizzically and raise an eyebrow. "I like that idea, but… aren't some things better in person?"

Hunter sighs and looks down at my calves again before he starts rubbing them. "Probably."

"Also, not to piss in your Cheerios, but we don't want this getting out. I mean, I trust my cousins and parents to keep it quiet, but if your parents and family wouldn't be accepting, do we want to take that risk?"

He leaves one hand on my leg and leans back groaning as he rubs his eyes. "You're right."

I lay back on his couch and close my eyes. "This isn't going to work, Hunter," I say quietly. "It's the best idea for me to quit the team. You were right. What we did was a huge mistake. I don't even know how I caught feelings so fast."

Hunter chuckles. I feel him shifting, but I don't dare open my eyes. Not even when I feel him lowering himself down on top of me. He holds part of his weight off me by settling his elbows and forearms on either side of my head.

"Look at me." His voice is dominant, and I can't help but obey. My eyes flutter open, but I don't dare move. I'm afraid he'll disappear if I do. That this will be nothing but a dream. "Firstly, this was not something that happened fast, Kody. Sure, we had a hell of a connection, but it's taken us a while to fall in love with each other. And we did that even though we've both been assholes towards each other."

I nod slowly. "You're right," I whisper. "I'm sorry."

He shakes his head and runs his fingers through my hair. "There's nothing to apologize for," he says soothingly. His words are like honey dripping into my soul to seal all of the chips and breaks. "Secondly, we need to be sure what we want goin' forward. I know what I want. I want you, and I'm not willing to fight that anymore. But it's not all about me."

"I want you. I want to be with you. More than anything. Being without you is too hard. I'm just afraid of how we're going to navigate this."

"We treat it like any other relationship minus the PDA. Date nights can be here. You've got access to the building. You can come over here anytime you want. I'll even get you a key."

My eyebrows shoot up. "You trust me enough to give me a key?"

He grins. "Why not? Ya have one to my office. You haven't fucked me over on that."

"I'd never do that."

"So, what'd you think?"

"I want this so much. It's all I've wanted for two years."

Hunter grins again, only wider this time. "Tell me I can kiss you now. I'm barely containing myself."

"Kiss me like it's our last time," I say, still not sure if it's going to be or not. I blink at the tears suddenly stinging my eyes. No fucking way am I crying in front of this man.

He leans down and brushes his lips across mine. "I'll kiss you like it's our first because there's many more to come now that we've gotten past this wall I put up to protect you."

And with that, his lips meet mine in a kiss just as fiery as the one in Black. We sink into each other as the kiss gets deeper. Our tongues entwine and clash. Our own unique tastes intermix with the other's. The difference is this time, we're not devouring each other's faces. It's slow, and while it's still hot, there's far more feelings being poured into it. Feelings that we've both shoved down for far too many minutes, hours, days, months… years…

I'd like to say I was a good boy and wrapped my arms around him in a cute little hug, but that's not what happened. I wrap my arms around him and pull him closer. I wrap my legs around his waist and force him to relieve the pressure in my dick with his weight.

But that never works.

It only makes the burning need I have for him stronger. Hotter. Before I know what I'm doing. I'm grinding against him, needing the friction he gives to relieve the pressure in my hard as fuck cock. Like a horny teenager, which I'm not far away from, I'm only twenty, I'm dry humping my coach like there's not going to be a tomorrow. I don't even care that I'm about to embarrass myself by coming in my jeans.

"Mmm…," Hunter moans into the kiss before pulling away just enough to give us both room to breathe.

"Mmm…" My moan comes out more of a growl because I want so much more. I'm pent up with so many emotions that I don't know how to deal with, and all I want is to feel every part of him fucking me hard enough to make me see stars while centering me at the same time.

"We need to slow down. We have all the time in the world." His voice is low and growly; filled with lust and desire. I can see the fire in his eyes and know it mirrors my own.

"I'm not above begging. I need you. I need to feel you. Taste you." I try to pull him down, but he holds firm. His eyes darken.

"When I fuck you again, boy, I'm taking my time. You're gonna feel me for days. We don't have that much time right now. I need all night and day to show you how much I missed you."

I feel the blush creeping up my neck and to my face. Suddenly, I know how Blade makes Drake feel, and I want that for the rest of my life.

With Hunter.

Am I crazy?

Yeah. Fucking certifiably insane, but I don't care. Being with Hunter makes me feel whole again. Like all of the darkness that entered my soul is finding the light again. Like the cracks in my carefully placed façade are being filled with him. I feel complete for the first time in my life. I found my person. The one who owns my heart, body, mind, and soul.

Too soon? Probably to some. I've been waiting for him for two years. Hell, my entire life. I don't want to be without him for another second. I need to feel that connection again.

But more than my own need, I trust him. I know he knows what's best, and if he says he needs more than just an hour to satisfy both of us, then I believe him.

He leans in and kisses me again, this time more tenderly. Lovingly, maybe? I can only dare to dream as I melt into him once more and send a plea to any God listening to let me keep him.

Chapter Five

☾ Hunter ☾

I sit down on one of the logs sitting around the firepit. I'm impressed. Brant made a couple of benches out of a couple logs. They're very comfortable and are perfect for company.

Across from me, Sterling is sitting next to a younger girl I recognize as his stepsister. She looks extremely nervous and uncomfortable, upset even, but the second he hugs her, she's far more calm. When he pulls away, she's smiling. I can't hear what he's saying, but he starts pointing out other players on the team and a few of the girls, Brant's girlfriend included. After a few moments, he's guiding her over to the group of girls, who are happily deep in conversation.

The party is going very well. Everyone is mingling. Brant had all the food catered. It was delicious, and there's still a lot left. He got BBQ. There's nothing better than a good ole Texas BBQ. Brisket, chicken, beef tips, even mac and cheese.

"Heads up, Coach!" one of my players yells from across the yard. I look up just in time to see a football flying directly at my head.

I stand and catch it with a grin. "Who the hell threw that so far out of bounds?"

"It was X!" another player, Danny, says with a laugh.

"It slipped!" Xavier barks with a sarcastic tone to his voice that makes me think the throw was intentional.

"Bullshit! You're the most accurate passer in the entirety of college football. That was intentional!" I yell back as I throw the ball to him.

"Oh shit!" Xavier says with a gleeful laugh. "Coach got an arm on him!"

"And don't you forget that!" I say teasingly.

They all laugh as they go back to their game. Kody glances at me before he ducks his head and gets back to his position on the makeshift field. I watch him because I can't take my eyes off him. He's mesmerizing. His field work is just a beautiful sight. I've seen him get the ball and take off. If he gets open, there's no one stopping him. He's fucking fast and as graceful as a damn gazelle.

I'm so wrapped in watching him, I don't notice that Sterling is standing next to me. "He's a good man, you know," he says, his deep voice rumbling.

I jump slightly and look at him. "Yeah. I know."

"What were you guys talking about after practice today? Whatever it was, it turned his mood around."

I smile and let out a small chuckle. "Good. He doesn't deserve to feel like he did ever again."

I see him nod out of the corner of my eye as he reaches behind him. I glance at him as he pulls something out of his jeans pocket. "You didn't get this from me." He hands me the folded paper, but when I try and take it, he doesn't let it go right away. "Take care of my cousin. He's been through a lot."

I glance down at the paper before looking up at Kody and then back at Sterling. I recognize the same protective look in his eyes that I often get in my own. He's very serious. "I will," I say low but resolutely.

He nods again and releases the paper after a few moments of a stare down. It's like he's making sure I'm not lying, and I wonder just how much he knows. Which makes me curious as to what all of them know. I know they're all as close as brothers.

Sterling strides off and picks up a nerf gun. I can't help but laugh and pick one up myself. I want to look at that paper, but I want to join in this team bonding. I put the paper in my back pocket and dart behind a tree. Sterling is behind another one and winks at me. He signals to the table of girls, and I immediately understand. He wants to attack them so the rest of the guys join in to defend them. I nod, and he takes aim at his stepsister.

I grin and take my aim at one I recognize as Danny's girlfriend. Sterling counts us down from three and we silently fire at the same time, hitting both girls in the back. At their shocked screams, all of the guys stop what they're doing and look at them as Sterling and I step out from behind the trees.

"Did… you just… start a nerf gun war?" Sloane, Brant's girlfriend, asks.

"Oh, fuck yes," Sterling answers with a wicked grin.

"Have you lost your mind? I haven't lost yet."

"Yeah, I know. That's why we didn't shoot you," Sterlings says with a grin. "Obviously, we need you on our team."

"And we promise to protect you with our lives," I chip in.

"Fuck that. Offer her a cookie. That'll get her," Sterling says.

"Cookie?" Sloane asks, looking at Sterling with wide eyes.

"No! Don't fall for that! We need you with us!" Brant yells as he picks up a nerf gun. "I'll give you anything you want." He gives her a look that I know damn well makes her panties wet. We definitely lost her.

"Can't resist that." She giggles and grabs another nerf gun.

Everyone chooses sides. I watch in disbelief and an open mouth when I see Kody standing next to Brant. He just gives me a wicked grin, and I know I'm in for it.

Once everyone chooses sides, Xavier speaks up, quieting everyone. He's a true leader, and I'm glad he chose my team. "Alright, everyone. We look pretty even. The rules to a nerf gun war are no being a dick, no violence, like shoving, punching, none of that shit, and treat this like a fun reprieve because that's what it is. Anyone who wants to test the rules faces me. Questions, comments, or concerns?"

"Nope! Let's get going so we can win!" Drake says. We all laugh.

"And go!" Xavier barks.

We all take off running. Everyone on my team is wearing a red flag. Everyone on Kody's team is wearing a yellow one. The goal is take out everyone on the opposite team. Once they're hit, we need to get their flag off. If we don't, they stay in. If we do, they move to the sidelines.

It sounds easy, but it's not. It's a constant game of dodging and strategy, which Sterling and I have going perfectly. He or I shoot, and the other one grabs the flag before dodging out of the way of becoming a potential target.

The game goes on for most of the rest of the night until it's just me against Kody and Sloane. I lost Sterling to a stray hit and perfectly placed lineman. Sloane and Kody both grin at me evilly after looking at each other. I know exactly what they're gonna try, but I'm still fast. They can shoot, but I can run.

What I don't count on is them having a strategy of their own. I know I'm in trouble the second Kody takes off running towards me. I turn quickly and sprint away, but I already know I'm not gonna make it. I feel the nerf hit dead center in my back, but I don't stop.

"Yeah! Get him, Kody! Go!" someone yells.

"He's almost got you, Coach!" another person yells at me. "Run! Go! Faster!"

I pump my legs harder, but it's no use. I still have my speed, but Kody isn't known as' bullet' by other teams for nothing. I sense he's close, so I try to dodge him, but he's expecting it and grabs my flag.

"Yeah!" everyone cheers, including those on my own team.

"Traitors!" I bark with a laugh.

"Can't help it, Coach!" Tyler, one of my backup quarterbacks, says. "It was fun seein' the great Hunter Steele get run down!"

I laugh as Kody and I walk back towards everyone else. "You're running laps. Ten sounds good."

Everyone laughs again.

"Alright, everyone!" Brant yells above the loud din. "Ready for the bonfire?"

A chorus of, "Hell ya!" courses through the night. Brant and Xavier light it up to more cheers. When Kody and I get closer, we claim a bench near the pit for ourselves.

"I had fun," Kody says with a smile as he looks at me.

I grin. "Me too."

We fall into a comfortable silence next to each other. After a few moments, I catch Sterling watching us. He gives me a nod, and I remember the paper he gave me. I reach in my pocket and feel it still there.

Making sure my voice is low, I lean into Kody a little, making sure only he can hear me. "Meet me inside the house." I say nothing more. Instead, I get up and wink at Sterling as I make my way into the house. He grins and winks back.

Once inside, I take out the paper and start reading it as I walk around to find a quiet place where no one can see me or notice me. I settle by the bar in the den and start reading. No windows here.

The more and more I read, the wider my eyes get. Sterling is a fucking genius. My grin grows and the dread I was feeling over the consequences of my relationship with Kody starts to wane more and more.

"Holy shit," I rumble outloud.

"What?" Kody says as he walks into the den.

I look at him with a huge smile on my face. "First off, I think your cousins know about you. And second, Sterling is a goddamn genius." I hand him the paper.

It's a copy of two pages of the employee handbook. I'm not gonna ask him how he got it. On the back side is a copy of two pages from the student handbook. As Kody reads them, I lean against the bar and watch him. Like me, his expression changes from wonder to happiness to pure delight when he finally meets my eyes.

"Relationships between students and staff isn't banned."

I nod my head. "Correct. Did you read the rest?"

"Yeah, but I don't know what it means."

"Basically, it means that should the relationship be brought to light by anyone else, the university will do an internal investigation. Should any kind of favoritism come out of the investigation, the university can take action against the staff member. But it explicitly states that the university believes in not dictatin' people's lives and won't do anything about the relationship as long as no wrongdoin' is occurring. Like not sharing test answers or not switching grades. Giving too much leeway. Askin' other teachers to give more favoritism to the student."

Kody's grin widens even more. "So, we can be together and not have to hide it?"

"Technically, yes. But before that happens, we have some things we need to do. Like tell the people who matter to us before going public. And then prepare for the storm that will come because the media will get a hold of this. We need to figure out just how far we're willin' to go with all this and how much we're willin' to talk about it."

Kody nods and steps closer to me. It's impossible for me to resist touching him, so I pull him close. But having my arms around him only does one thing. Trying to keep my dick at bay, I attempt to satiate it enough with a kiss that quickly goes out of control.

"Hunter," Kody moans against my lips as he rubs his dick against mine. The jeans we're wearing are far too fucking much fabric between us, and the only thing I can think of is getting them off.

I should back away, but I don't. Instead, I grip his tight ass and lift him off the ground, forcing him to jump a little for me so I can grip him properly when I slam him against the wall.

I realize far too late, I didn't pull his jeans or mine down first. "Fuck." I let him down and immediately undo his belt and button on his jeans. I push them down in a hurry, my lips not leaving his for a second.

Once his are down, I work on mine. Kody manages to get his off without breaking our kiss. I push mine down enough to free my dick before I have him in my arms again. His legs wrap around my waist, his arms around my shoulders, and I deepen the kiss just as I slam my cock home.

"Oh fuck, daddy," Kody groans as he nips my bottom lip.

I didn't think it was possible to get harder, but him remembering my bedroom preference turns my dick to steel. "I've missed this tight little hole."

"All for you," he says, looking me directly in my eyes.

I growl possessively. "All fucking mine, my boy." I start thrusting slow and hard so he feels every ridge and vein my dick has.

"All… yours…," he says to the rhythm of my hard thrusts.

I kiss down his jaw to his neck. "I'm not lasting long, my boy. Stroke your dick for me."

"Yes, daddy." Trusting me to hold his weight and without hesitation, he releases my shoulders with one arm and starts jacking himself.

"Fuck, that's the hottest thing I've ever seen." I kiss his neck, biting it lightly before sucking. I'm marking him. Everyone needs to know he belongs to me. "Keep it up, baby."

His eyes roll back in his head. I don't pick up my pace because I need to feel him squeezing me with every thrust I give him. I need him to feel all he does to me. I need us both to enjoy this for as long as we can because we both need to release the pent up sexual frustration we have. Just as he's not been with anyone else, neither have I. No one could possibly compare to him, but what's more is that I didn't want anyone else. One taste of him fucked me up for anyone else.

I thrust up into him, hitting his prostate until he's about to come and writhing for that release. Unable to hold back, I fill his ass with enough come that it's leaking out of him as my body trembles. "Fuck, boy. Oh fuck, baby."

"I'm gonna... I can't... Daddy!" Kody throws his head back against the wall as he gasps. Like the good boy he is, he hasn't quit stroking his dick.

I pull out of him, even though I really don't want to. I can't let my boy suffer. I set him down on his feet and kneel in front of him. I grip his wrist and take the place of his hand with my mouth. With my other hand, I play with his balls and scrape my bottom teeth along the vein on the underside of his dick. It's all it takes for him to lose control.

He slaps his hand over his mouth and thrusts into mine. "Daddy!" he shouts.

I swallow around him and drink his come like it's my favorite drink.

And it is.

He sinks to his knees as we both come down. I wrap my arms around him and hold him tight just as I wanted to do the night in the club that changed both our lives.

Chapter Six

☪ Kody ☪

(Two Weeks Later)

I pace in the locker room after getting dressed. Hunter is with another player in his office, and I'm getting more and more nervous. We picked today to tell my family and parents about my sexuality. We told his already, and it went about as well as he expected. I hate that he has to go through that. I know in my heart my family will be accepting of me and him as being gay, but I don't know how anyone will feel when we tell them we're together, which is our plan.

We didn't tell his family that little tidbit. Hunter was convinced they'd make trouble for us. After hearing the horrible things they said to him, I couldn't have possibly agreed more with the decision he made, though I would've agreed anyway with whatever he wanted to do.

On my umpteenth lap around the locker room, Hunter's door finally opens. I stop pacing as Adrian, our center steps out.

"Thanks, Coach."

"Anytime. Never hesitate to reach out. I got your back."

I don't say anything, but I know he's been struggling in his English class. It's boring for him. He was forced to take it. They won't let him test out of it, but he should be in a more advanced class. He's completed all of his work for the entire semester, it was all listed on a very detailed seventeen page syllabus, and simply doesn't show up for class. The instructor changed the rules and started making attendance count as part of the grade. Adrian is failing the class because he's only shown up four times the entire term so far. We're close to midterms, and the professor is pissed.

I happen to know because I'm in his class. If he fails, he's off the team. I told him to talk to Hunter because I knew he'd be able to figure something out.

"Thanks, man," Adrian says to me with a nod as he walks by me.

"Anytime."

Hunter is leaning against his office door frame with his arms crossed over his chest and one leg crossed over the other. He watches Adrian leave. Once he's gone, his hungry eyes turn to me, making me melt.

"Ready to do this?" he asks. I love his deep Southern drawl.

"And all at once, my hardening dick is deflating like a fucking balloon."

Hunter laughs. "I'll make it up to you. Did you drive here?"

"I came with Drake on his bike. So, I'll just ride with you, if that's okay." Suddenly, my heart starts racing. "Shit. I assumed it would be okay. I should've asked first. I can grab an Ub-"

"You're not grabbin' an Uber." Hunter pushes off the door frame and disappears in his office. He's back seconds later and closing his door. "What the hell kind of boyfriend would I be if I just let ya take an Uber when I'm here?"

I blush. "Boyfriend?" It's the first time he's said it.

He stops in front of me. His hand moves to my throat before sliding around to the back of my neck. He leans in and kisses me. The feel of his rough and calloused fingers sends shivers down my spine, but it's the hard kiss that has me groaning and adjusting myself.

He pulls away from the kiss far too late. My insides feel like he's seared them. Now, I need him to fix me so I keep breathing.

"Yes. Boyfriend. Pretty sure I made that clear over the past couple weeks. You belong to me. You're mine. Not just in the bedroom. Mine completely and all it encompasses."

I grin as his words seep in and heal me in more ways than he'll ever understand. "Yes, sir."

He growls with a teasing grin before swatting my ass. "Let's go before I fuck you on my desk again."

"That was fun. I'll take that deal."

Hunter laughs and takes my hand. He pulls me with him out of the locker room before squeezing my hand and letting it go. We've decided keeping things under the radar is the best thing for now. There are no repercussions that would come to me when it comes to any NFL team or the university itself, but we still don't want any drama. What we do outside the school walls is our own business. Neither of us are big fans of dates out anyway. We prefer pizza and movie nights.

We've gotten to know a lot about each other over the past couple of years. We've had team building exercises a lot because Hunter feels they're important. The more we've done, the more I believe him. But over the past couple of weeks, we've gotten to know each other a lot more deeply. I've spent a lot of time at his penthouse. My cousins and parents have started to ask questions. I don't like lying to them. I've been saying I've been going to see a friend and hang out with him, but that only flew for so long.

Once we're settled in Hunter's truck I lean my head back against the seat. "I don't like not knowing what to expect."

"I think ya know what to expect, though. You're just fightin' it because you're scared. Which is okay. It's okay to fear somethin' like this. I'm not sayin' it ain't. I just think you know what to expect and should focus your attention on that."

Hunter pulls out of the parking lot and drives towards my house. The closer we get, the faster my heart races. When we're a block away, Hunter pulls over and takes my hand in his as he turns towards me. I look at him. I'm starting to panic. I can feel it.

"Look at me, baby." His voice is dominant. The tone I need right now. The one that forces me to listen but is still soothing and calming. I don't know how he does it.

I look at him, my lip trembling. "I -"

"Shh… Listen to me." He takes my other hand in his and brings them both to his lips to kiss. "I know you're scared. But I'm here. I'm right here. I'm not goin' anywhere no matter what happens in there. I believe wholeheartedly that everythin's gonna be just fine. I know your cousins well enough and have observed them enough to know how protective they are. And how acceptin' they are. And how lovin' they are. How important family is. I don't doubt your parents are the same way."

"They are. I know they are. What if they hate me for not telling them sooner? What if -"

He cuts me off by kissing me. "No what ifs," he says when he pulls away. "We're gonna go in there. And we're doin' this together. Just like I promised." He squeezes my hands.

"Maybe we could wait."

"No."

"But -"

"No, Kody. We're goin'. Right now." He kisses me as he lets go of my hands. He turns in his seat and puts his truck in gear.

I know better than to argue, but by the time we get to my house, I'm thinking of all the reasons this is a terrible idea.

"I don't want to do this now."

"If you don't, you're goin' over my knee. I understand you're scared of the reaction, but you need to trust me, my boy." He jumps down from his truck and strides to my door. He opens it. "Are you gettin' out? Or am I throwin' you over my shoulder?"

My eyes widen at his tone. I immediately jump down with no argument. I don't doubt for a minute that he'd do exactly as he said. Walking in over his shoulder is certainly not how I want to tell them.

"Okay, okay."

"Good boy. Don't get sassy like that again. I only give one warning. Next time, it's five spankings."

I bite my lip and look up at him through my lashes as I blush. "That doesn't sound like fun."

"Not meant to be." He leans down so his lips are just a breath from mine. "But I can make it fun." His voice is dangerous.

I almost giggle but grin instead before taking a breath. "Okay. We're doing this. Can you stay out by the door? I want to make sure everyone is there and in the same room. Then, I want to go in holding hands. If that's okay."

"If that's what my boy wants, it's what he gets."

I grin and head into the house while he waits outside on the patio. Once I have the door closed behind me, I start taking off my shoes.

"Kody?" my dad calls as he comes around the corner.

I smile and hug him. "Hey, dad. How was your trip?"

He hugs me back, and I grip him a little tighter. I don't know why but I feel like I needed this. "It was good, big man. I hated I had to miss your game last week. Second one I've ever missed, and I felt just as bad as the first game."

I laugh as I pull away. "That was when I was like eight."

"Still hurt to miss it." He looks over his shoulder. "There's a lot of people here. Your mom said they ain't for me. What's going on?"

The nerves immediately hit me hard again. I can't help but rub my chest to relieve the ache. "Uh. Well, I have some pretty big stuff to share. I wanted everyone here."

"That big, huh?"

"Yeah, pretty earth shattering. I don't know how people are gonna take it." I look down at my feet.

My dad puts his hand on my shoulder. "Whatever it is, we're all here for you." He pats my back.

"Can you just make sure everyone is in the living room?"

"Yep. I'll take care of it." He turns and heads towards our living room.

I take a deep breath before I make my way back to Hunter. Once I open the door, the sight I'm greeted with is breathtaking. Hunter is leaning against a pillar. When I open the door, his smile stops my heart.

"Ready?" he drawls.

I nod. I don't think I can actually talk right now. Thankfully, he doesn't make me. He just walks towards me and takes my hand. He allows me to lead him inside. I don't let go of his hand as he slides his shoes off. I don't think I could let go anyway. He doesn't know it, but he's my anchor. He's keeping from avoiding this whole thing and running.

Why is this so hard? It's not like anyone is going to shun me. They've proven that time and time again. Stop being a baby, Kody. If Hunter can do this, so can you. You need to prove your worth to him.

Where the hell did that come from? I growl at myself, but there's a deeply seated need to make him see my worth. To have to prove it to him. I know better. I know I'm worthy, but that doesn't stop those intrusive thoughts from entering my mind.

As if he knows what's going on in my mind, Hunter squeezes my hand as he nudges me forward. I hadn't even realized I stopped walking.

I glance at him, and his smile gives me the confidence I'm very much lacking. I force myself to breathe. Once we get to the living room, I'm immediately attacked by two screaming girls.

"Kody!" Dylan and Rosie both squeal as they leap at me. I have to drop Hunter's hand just to keep us all from tumbling to the ground.

Once I steady us, I hug them both. "I've missed you guys. What are you doing here?"

"X texted and said you have some news and need the family," Dylan says as she looks up at me.

"So, we asked Cole if he'd come down with us," Rosie finishes as she points to Cole.

I nod with a grin. Cole is Dylan's boyfriend. Her and Rosie live in Chicago now, so we don't get to see them as much, but I'm happy Xavier texted them. I've missed them and am excited to see them. "I'm glad y'all are here," I tell them.

They both give me a final squeeze and smile before they walk back into the living room to join everyone. Sterling's parents are here. All of my cousins are scattered in the room. Sloane and Colton are here. Blade is here. My parents are happily seated and obviously excited that we're all under one roof.

I clear my throat nervously, completely unsure if I want to stand or sit while doing this. Hunter moves closer and takes my hand once more. I look up at him, holding my breath.

"We got this," he whispers.

"Can you start...?" I ask hopefully.

Hunter smiles. "Yes, but I'm not sharing everything. This is your story." He squeezes my hand and looks at everyone. "Everyone. We have something we'd like to share. But first, Kody has something to tell everyone." He squeezes my hand again. His voice is deep. Dominant. Everything I need right now to calm me.

I take one more deep, calming breath and focus on the contact Hunter is giving me. "I'm gay," I blurt out before I can think about and stop myself. I stare at everyone with wide eyes as they look at each other.

Sterling's parents seem to be fighting glares. That doesn't surprise me. I've never liked them anyway. There's something so fucked up about them. Everyone else is smiling at me. Dylan has tears in her eyes.

It's my mother who breaks the deafening silence. "Oh, honey." She stands and walks to me. She hugs me, but I only hug her back with one arm. I can't let go of Hunter's hand. Not until I get one more person's approval.

My eyes meet my dad's as he stands. "I assume the rest is that you and Coach Steele are a couple?"

I can't find the words. Tears sting my eyes. I just nod.

"Yes, sir, we are," Hunter says, saving me. "I checked the policies with the university, and there's nothing wrong with us being together. It's not against policy."

My dad nods and looks at me as my mom releases me. His expression gives nothing away. I don't know if he's mad or not. "This is where you've been going?"

"Yes, sir." I swallow hard.

My dad nods again before hugging me. "I'm happy for you."

I damn near slump into him, but still refuse to let go of Hunter's hand. I'm holding it in a death grip, but he's keeping my heart from ending up in my mouth. He's my solid ground.

"'Bout damn time y'all come out and admit your attraction," Drake says with a smirk as my dad pulls away. The entire room erupts in laughter, but Hunter and I just look at each other.

"What are you talking about?" I finally ask, looking at Drake.

"Come on, man," Brant says. "If you think we didn't know the second you guys saw each other that something was up, you don't know us too well."

"That sexual tension is off the fucking charts," Xavier chips in. Everyone laughs again. Even Hunter and I join.

Hunter leads me to an open oversized chair and sits down, pulling me down next to him so I'm half on his lap. "Was it that obvious?" he rumbles as he puts his arm around me.

"You could've lit the field on fire. We're all shocked you didn't," Sterling says with his signature smirk.

"Point taken," I say with a laugh.

After spending some time talking, my dad starts up the grill with Sterling's dad. We all move outside and lounge around the pool just talking, and I've never felt more at peace.

I feel complete for the first time in longer than I can even remember.

I feel whole.

Chapter Seven

☪ Hunter ☪

(One Month Later)

At exactly 4:15pm, I walk into the Administration Office for a meeting I'm not at all excited about. Cutting practice two days before an insanely important game and being forced to take one of my best players with me simply pisses me off.

I stop at the Administration desk. "Appointment with the Dean. Kody Remington and Coach Steele."

The secretary, a fairly young person probably working her way through college, glares up at me, but when she sees who I am, her expression completely changes. "Coach Steele! Hey! The Dean is expecting you. Go on back."

I chuckle at the barely perceptible growl that comes out of Kody. I see him glare out of the corner of my eye. I look at him and tilt my head to the side so he follows me. He does as I wordlessly command. When we reach the Dean's office I step inside. His door is already open.

"Dean Martinez," I say, announcing our presence.

"Come in. Close the door." He looks up at us both as we step in. He's a man of around five feet ten inches. He's getting up there in age, but he's still very kind, yet commanding. I close the door, and Kody and I both sit. "Look. I'm cutting straight to the chase. I got some pictures. Before I even share them, I want you to know that I'm on your side. Student and faculty policy doesn't have anything to say against relationships as long as said relationship remains moral and ethical. So, I need to know. Are the two of you together?"

I can't help the glare that reaches my eyes. Kody stays silent with his head down. "You made me cancel practice for this?"

Dean Martinez has the decency to look a little shocked. "I didn't think about it. I apologize."

I sigh. "Yes. We're dating. No. We haven't done anything even remotely unethical. We don't even hold hands on campus. We made the mutual decision to keep things separate."

It's true. I haven't fucked him on my desk or in my office since the first couple of times it was done. We haven't even kissed or held hands here since the day we left the locker room to tell his family about his sexuality and our relationship.

Dean Martinez opens a folder with pictures of Kody and I locked in an embrace, and it infuriates me that someone is taking that moment out of context.

Kody looks at me, fear in his eyes, and I'm instantly more angry that he was even put in a situation where he has to feel like that.

"Kody was having a very, very rough day. He broke down. What the hell was I supposed to do? Leave him to fight alone? Sometimes, guys need a hug, too. That was before we were even officially discussing our relationship."

"Understandable. Again, I have no issue with that. This is for you and Kody so you are aware. The university is willing to defend you if something comes up, but if that happens, you have to be aware of the drama. I don't want this coming out and shocking you." He flips the pic over to reveal another one.

Kody gasps. "Sir, that's not even on campus! That's outside my house."

"Who sent this?" I ask. The picture is of Kody taking my hand and leading me into his house. There are others of me standing outside. "It looks like the obsession is with me."

"I don't know who sent them in, but this is a head's up." Dean Martinez stands. "Do with that what you will, gentlemen. In the meantime, no policies have been broken." He opens the door to his office.

I look at Kody as I grab the folder. His eyes are locked on images. When I close the folder, his eyes snap to mine before he stands. I narrow mine. I know he saw something in those images I didn't and has information he doesn't want to tell me here.

I lead him out of the office and wait until we're outside before I dare ask. "What did you see? Something I didn't? Do you know who it is or have an idea?"

He nods but says nothing as he looks around. "I need to figure a few things out," he says to me. "I'll meet you at your penthouse." He starts to beeline for the parking lot, but I grab his wrist. I don't care who sees me.

"Talk to me."

"I have to talk to my cousins first, Hunter. Please. Just trust me on this. I'll meet you at your penthouse."

I let go of his wrist, but I don't want to. "Can you at least give me a hint so I know you're not in danger?"

He looks down at the ground. He does it when he needs to compose himself. He looks back up at me after a few moments. "I can't really promise I'm not. I have an idea of who did it, and it just put a couple other things into perspective for me. I have to talk to my cousins."

"Then, I'm going with you." I can't even begin to tell him how panicked I am.

"No, Hunter. I got this. I promise."

"You can't promise me you're safe. There's no way I'm letting you go without me."

I see the second he gives in. Instead of walking towards his car, he turns and starts walking to the lot behind the stadium where I park. I fall into step with him.

"You're gonna make me explain, aren't you?"

"Damn right."

Kody sighs. "Some things have been going on lately that have both Colton and Blade on edge. You know Colton is a cop. I don't know how much you know about Blade, but he's the President of Viper's Venom. They're a dangerous as hell motorcycle crew. They're bigger than Hell's Angels. What sets them apart is that they're legal. They help the cops. And probably do things they shouldn't that the cops legally can't. Long story short, there was a lot of stuff going down with a trafficking ring here. Blade and Colton heard about it. Now they're doing all this digging. They're uncovering a lot of stuff, but not exactly how these women are vanishing. There has to be a path. A trail. An underground railroad, if I can use that as an example. It's hidden, but it's there."

"Okay, so what does all of that have to do with you and what you saw?"

"I think I know who took those pics. In that last pic, there was a reflection in the truck mirror. I recognize the truck. Didn't you?"

I look down at him with furrowed brows. "I'm supposed to?"

"Well, I'd think you would. You probably will once I tell you who it is."

"Okay, who is it?" We stop at my truck, and he pauses with his hand on the door handle.

He turns and looks up at me. "Sterling."

My eyes nearly bulge out of my head. "You're kidding. Are you suggesting your cousin took those pics and turned them in anonymously to the Dean? That doesn't seem like him."

Kody opens the door and climbs in. "Not him." He looks down at me as he puts his seatbelt on. "His stepsister."

I nearly choke before closing the door. I climb into my truck and start it. I put it in gear and pull out of the lot before I say a word. "How do you know?"

"I suspect. I don't know. I have to talk to my cousins. And Colton. Colton especially. We need to go to his and Xavier's place."

I watch him as he starts furiously typing on his phone as I drive.

I don't know what's going on, but I'm very much on edge.

Chapter Eight

☪ Kody ☪

"So, you really think there's a traffickin' ring going on that involves your uncle?" Hunter asks me as we turn into Sterling's driveway.

His house is one of the biggest I've ever seen. My parents have money, but Sterling's tops us all. His parents are richer than Dylan's were, and Dylan's dad was a Senator. I say was because they are both long gone. They were the sickest people I've ever known, and I couldn't be happier that the Crane and Lucinio Mafias took them down. Dylan, my cousin, is safe from her parents now and any other danger they threw her in.

Though, if I'm onto what I think I am, Sterling's parents take the crown in the sickest of everyone in the Remington family.

"Yeah. But before he gets ambushed, I need to talk to him." I look at Hunter. "Wait here. I promise I'll be okay in there. Give me ten minutes before you charge in there."

"Five."

"Done."

I jump quickly out of his truck because his tone leaves no room for any kind of argument. I know him well enough to know he'll storm in if I'm not out here in five minutes. He's incredibly protective, and he thinks I'm in danger right now.

If what I'm thinking is right, he's not wrong.

Without knocking, I enter Sterling's family home. We rarely ever knock on each other's house door, but we've started to with Xavier and Colton, Drake and Blade, and Brant and Sloane because we never know what we're going to be walking into if we don't.

The thought makes me chuckle, but I stop quickly when I hear Sterling's low voice coming from the hallway near me. I listen as I lightly close the door.

"I promise, Riley. I'll get you out. I promise. But I can't do anything for a couple weeks. He can have me arrested."

"But he won't. He loves you. You're his pride and joy. Please just get me out. I don't know what he'll do next," Riley, Sterling's stepsister, says. I can hear the tears in her eyes, and it makes me want to hug her, but I don't know what's happening.

"Please don't cry. I'll do whatever I can, okay? Come here."

I peak around the corner just as Sterling pulls Riley into his arms. She breaks down in sobs in his arms as I clear my throat. "Hey," I say quietly.

Riley hides in Sterling and tries to wipe her eyes before I see her. Sterling, to his credit, just hugs her tighter as he looks at me. "Hey."

"Uh, look, I have the guys getting together at X's house. I know your car's in the shop. Thought I'd pick you up. It's important."

Keeping one arm around Riley, he runs his fingers through his hair. "Yeah. I'll come, but Riley needs to come with. She has some homework, so she can do it in the den or something."

I nod. "That's fine."

"I can't go," Riley whispers.

Sterling looks down at her but still hugs her, even though she pulls back. "Why?"

"I'm grounded, Sterling. Remember?"

Sterling and I both sigh. I meet his eyes. They're dark. Almost as black as Satan's soul. I rub a hand down my face. My five minutes are almost up. Any second now, Hunter is coming in.

"We gotta go, man," I say, but I absolutely am in agreement with him. Something is going on here, and I don't want Riley in the middle.

Sterling looks down at Riley once more and gives her a confident smile. "Go to your room. Lock it. If things get out of hand, you do what we talked about, right?"

Riley nods, teary. "Yes, sir."

"I taught you how to ride well enough to handle the green Ninja. Remember where the keys are?"

"Um…" She hesitates before looking at me then back to Sterling before shaking her head and looking down.

Sterling guides her face up with his thumb and forefinger so she's forced to look at him. "My closet. The white shoebox near the bottom of the shoebox stack. It's the only box without a pair of shoes. The key is in the tissue paper. Get them first, then go to your room. Do you remember where to go when you get out?"

"To Viper's Venom's Den. Anyone there will help."

"Good girl." Sterling hugs her again. I've always been able to see the bond they share, but something is very different now. "I'm a phone call or text away. I'll be back as soon as I can. And I'll stay here with you until you're eighteen. I'll drive you to school. Pick you up. I'll keep you with me on campus if I have practice or something. Okay? I won't leave you alone with him."

She nods as she lets him go. "Please don't be long," she whispers.

We all turn when we hear the door open. Riley's eyes light up with complete fear, and I wonder if I'm onto something that's bigger than I think.

"Riley!" Jacob Remington, my uncle, Sterling's dad, and Riley's stepdad, bellows into the hallway. He doesn't sound happy.

Sterling moves her behind him, and I follow his lead. We step out of the hallway. Uncle Jacob glares daggers through us both when he sees Riley behind him. From over Jacob's shoulder, I see Hunter appear in the doorway. He stays there like the backup I'm not sure we'll need.

"She's sick, dad," Sterling growls dangerously. I'd shiver at his tone if I hadn't heard it before. Sterling is the most protective out of all of us, though, most think it's Xavier. It's always been Sterling. "She'll be in her room with her door locked doing homework for the rest of the night. I'll bring her soup when I get back for dinner. No one needs to disturb her. Let her be."

Jacob glares. "Did you do your chores, Riley?" He folds his arms over his chest.

He's not as tall as me, Sterling, or Hunter. In fact, he's the shortest of all his brothers, and it's always been something that's chapped his ass. He uses his CEO status to intimidate everyone, but he's never been able to intimidate any of us.

"U-um…" Riley cowers behind Sterling, and I can see Hunter ready to pounce. Jacob has no idea Hunter is even behind him. If he does, he's doing a hell of a job at ignoring him completely.

"We'll do them," I say. "Me and Sterling. Riley really isn't in any condition to do anything but lay down."

Jacob's eyes flick between the two of us before settling on Sterling. "You have until ten. If they aren't done by then, there will be consequences for the both of you." He looks at me. "And I'll talk to Emerson about you. Either you obey, or I'll happily make you."

I roll my eyes and subtly wave Hunter off. His eyes turn to ice, as he shoots daggers into Jacob's back. He definitely didn't like that statement.

Without a word to him, I shake my head at my uncle and walk towards the stairs. Sterling keeps Riley behind him until he passes Jacob, then pulls her in front of him so she's in between me and Sterling on the way up the stairs. Hunter stays right where he is. When Jacob turns around and sees him, it's like a personality switch.

"Coach Steele! How are you?"

"Great," Hunter rumbles. I can hear the dominance in his voice. He's asserting his control over Jacob. "We have a quick meetin' about the upcoming game. Sterling said his car was out of commission, so me and Kody swung by on the way." A smooth lie that makes me grin.

"That's nice of you."

Their voices fade out as I lead Riley and Sterling to Riley's room. I turn towards them after opening Riley's door. I wait by the door and face the stairs as Sterling follows her in.

"Remember. Door locked. Out the window if he starts banging on your door. I'll get my keys."

Riley nods as Sterling jogs to his room. Riley lets out a breath as she sits at her desk. She turns on her laptop, then starts pulling out her homework and setting the books on her desk as she waits for her laptop to turn on.

"It's gonna be okay," I say reassuringly.

"I know," she says quietly.

Sterling comes up behind me, and I move so he can get by me. "Coach Steele has Jacob in a chokehold of a conversation," Sterling says. "Here's the keys to the bike. Don't hesitate. Just leave. He has no reason to come up here and bother you, and I'll reiterate that on my way out."

"Yes, sir," Riley whispers.

Sterling leans down and hugs her before whispering something in her ear. She smiles, although sadly, as he stands and walks towards me. She gets up and follows. Sterling closes the door and waits until we hear the door lock click into place. We both distinctly hear her crying as we walk away. It breaks my heart. Seeing what I just saw, I'm sure it destroys him.

Once we reach the bottom of the stairs, Sterling cuts the conversation his dad is having with Hunter off without a second thought. "Leave her alone, dad. I mean it. She's sick."

Jacob glares at him but does himself a solid by not saying a word and just nodding. Sterling is vibrating with anger. I can sense it.

We both follow Hunter outside and don't talk until we're in his truck and on the way to Xavier's and Colton's.

"Y'all need to tell me what the fuck is happenin' right now," Hunter says low and dominantly, almost dangerously.

I glance back at Sterling, who has his eyebrow raised. I take a deep breath. "I'll go first. I think we need to have everyone around, though."

"We can repeat it. This is already out of hand," Hunter responds, glancing at me.

I rub my temple and focus on the road. "Those pictures." I hand the folder back to Sterling to see. "They were taken by Riley. The shirt she's wearing is the same shirt she wore the night at my house when I came out. I know it's hers because it's her favorite one."

"I gave it to her for her birthday a couple of years ago. It's her for sure, but what the fuck does this mean? Where did you get these?" Sterling asks.

"We had a meetin' with the Dean of the University today," Hunter says. "He gave us that. Said it was sent anonymously."

"No," Sterling says more firmly. "Riley would never do that. She's taking the pics, obviously, but she'd never do anything like turn them in with the intention to harm anyone. This doesn't make sense. I'll talk to her. Get to the bottom of it."

"How do you know it's her?" Hunter asks.

"Good question." I smile weakly. "That shirt. It's custom. Sterling had it made especially for her. I know lots of people have shirts that say 'Pookie', but that one is one of a kind. It's her favorite color, magenta. And the 'Pookie' is in black, also her favorite color, but a special font that looks like blood. He did that because she loves horror movies and thrillers."

Hunter nods before sighing deeply. "I don't understand why. And how did you put this together with whatever else is going on? It seemed like this is somethin' major that has somethin' to do with what Colton's working on."

"Yeah." I look down at the floor. "Did anyone notice the tattoo on the under part of her wrist in the reflection?"

Sterling rumbles low. "Yeah. I was there when she got it. It's a rose."

"Oh fuck," Hunter breathes.

"What? Wha'd I miss?" Sterling asks.

I hate myself for what I'm about to say. "The single red rose. Britney Spears conspiracy theorists believed that her coming out with all of these rose emojis and hiding them in her posts and stuff on social media was a sign that she needed help. That she was being trafficked. I don't know how true it ended up being, but it gained a lot of ground. It was proven by some, disproven by others. One commonality was how crazy it made her look. I heard Blade and Colt talking about it, though. They were talking about how it became such a crazy phenomenon that this group they are after, this sex trafficking ring, seems to have some kind of an association with it. Every person they've found, alive or dead, has that tattoo. They don't know if they were calling for help, or being branded."

"We need to go back," Sterling says, panicked. "At least I do."

"I thought we should see what Colton has to say." I turn towards him. "And Blade. Maybe it's not what I'm thinking."

I've never seen Sterling look as freaked out as he does now. "I need to get to her, man. I'm not leaving her there alone if what you're thinking holds any kind of truth to it."

"I have to agree with him, Kody." Hunter makes a quick turn and makes his way quickly back to Sterling's house. "I get where you were comin' from, baby, but he's right. I don't think it's a good idea to leave her alone. We need to talk about gettin' her some kind of protection."

Hunter speeds through the streets as I chew my cheek and look out the window. I know they're right. I don't know what I was thinking. I should've just talked to Sterling at his house. It was stupid to have him leave. Especially since I sense so much danger.

I just hope Riley is okay.

Hopefully my fuck up didn't cause harm to her…

Chapter Nine

☾ Hunter ☾

(Two Days Later)

"Fuck," I rumble low when I see what's about to happen. It's a good thing they mic up college quarterbacks just like they do pro ones. "Switch the play, X," I say, holding a folder in front of my face so the coach for the Florida Gators doesn't see what I'm saying. "Shotgun to Sterling."

I see Xavier's head pop up. His hand comes up like he's signaling stop before he closes it into a fist. It means he agrees with the play, but not to who I want him to throw to. "Kill! Kill!" Xavier calls. "Red! Seven-zero. R! Line! Red! Seven-zero! R! Line! Hut! Hut! Hike!"

I grin. Xavier mixes football language in with his own codes. It's one of the things that makes him such a good quarterback. No one knows what the fuck to expect from him. He just told our players that he's changing the play on the line. He used Kody's favorite color and jersey number, backwards, to tell everyone he's throwing to him, all while telling Kody that he's throwing to him and to be at the right sideline.

The offensive line doesn't move at all. We don't want the Gators' defensive line to be able to adjust to the new play called. Our offensive line, though, knows exactly what to do. They know they need to protect both Xavier and Kody.

The second the ball snaps, it looks like pandemonium to the untrained eye. I can hear the gasps coming from the fans, but I smile. The players on the sidelines cheer. The line switches so all of our wide receivers become blockers. Sterling blocks for Kody before breaking free and running towards the sidelines towards Kody just as Xavier perfectly executes a spiral directly into Kody's waiting hands.

The crowd erupts into cheers. Out of the corner of my eye, I can see them standing up and jumping up and down, but my eyes are on my boy. Once Kody gets the ball, there's no one stopping him. He's too tough and fast. He can run through tackles just as well as he can dodge them.

So, when he catches the ball and takes off behind Sterling, I know there's no way anyone's stopping him.

"Yeah!" Brandon, one of the defensive lineman says. "Go, Kodeman!"

I run down the sidelines behind a few other players. The Gators' defense is doing their best to catch him, but Kody is at least five yards ahead of anyone else. The closest one to him gets blocked by Sterling, who is quickly replaced by two others defending Kody. The lead Kody has on everyone is increasing.

I glance up at the clock as I yell, "Run, Remington! Go! Open field!"

Four seconds.

Kody has fifteen yards to go before the endzone. A touchdown will win us the game by three points. We're currently down by three. Twenty-seven is what the Gators have. We have twenty-four and home field advantage. None of us want to be beat by Florida, or any other team, on our own turf.

Fuck that.

And it looks like our team agrees. Kody reaches the endzone, and the stadium sounds like it's roaring. This game was a hard fought win I knew we'd get, but these guys played hard and left it all on the field. I couldn't possibly be more proud.

Especially since this game just put us in the number one spot in rankings.

"Yeah!" Xavier yells when he reaches the endzone. He wraps his arms around Kody and lifts him clear off his feet. "Nice fucking run, 'cos!"

Kody grins as he takes his helmet off. "Nice audible, QB1!"

I'm just about to congratulate Kody when Xavier puts him down, but Kody's eyes widen. It's too late for me to realize what's going on and that that was his warning to me. Suddenly, an entire cooler of Gatorade is sloshing over my head, effectively soaking me from head to toe, even though I duck.

I laugh as I turn. Drake and Jack, another lineman, both laugh as they take off running with the cooler, but I get distracted from chasing them when I feel Kody's hand on my back as he appears at my side.

"How'd I do, Coach?" He winks, and the sass behind his eyes forces me to shift so no one sees what he's doing to me.

"Incredible run, Remington. Maybe next time, give 'em a chance to catch up, huh? Make it a game. At least a little."

Kody laughs. "Right. I'll be sure to do that next time." He winks as he joins his teammates.

My mouth drops. "Don't you dare! You'll give me a damn heart attack! Is that what you want?"

I hear Kody's laughter echoing as he disappears into the crowd of players and some students who were let onto the field. I do my usual congratulatory handshakes to the other coaches and players from the opposing side. I talk to the Gators' Head Coach for a few minutes while the teams themselves wish each other the best. The Gators are disappointed, rightfully so, but still good sports. They're one of my favorite teams to play.

It seems like it takes hours before I have Kody alone. After the game, we usually end up going out or to someone's house and ordering pizza to hang out and talk about the game and performance. It's another great team builder that I learned and took with me.

So, when I finally get my door unlocked and pull Kody into my penthouse, it takes very little time locking the door and having Kody's legs wrapped around my waist with my tongue down his throat like my cock is about to be. I carry him to the bedroom.

"Fuck, I've wanted to do that for hours," I growl possessively against his lips before claiming them with mine again. "I'm gonna fuck you until you can't walk."

He tugs my lower lip between his teeth with a low growl. "Make me feel you for days, daddy."

I grin. He knows damn well how much that turns me on, but I love every time he does it more and more because it means my good boy follows directions as well as he takes my dick. "Is my boy gonna be good and ride me?" I toss him on the bed the second I reach it.

He bounces a little bit with a groan before he's instantly on his knees. "Anything you want, daddy. I'm your good boy."

"Holy fuck."

I want to strip my clothes and sink deep into him, but I'm not like that. No. I need him to be all needy and ready for me. Hard as granite. Right on the brink of exploding for me; making a mess of me and the bed.

So, instead of stripping myself, I strip him. Slowly. Sensually. Despite the fact that my dick is screaming for release from the constraints of my pants, I run my fingers all over his body. Slowly. By the time I'm done, he's whimpering and moaning; arching off the bed.

When he moves his arms in an attempt to wrap around me, I straddle him and take off my tie. He looks at me curiously, and I grin. I tie his hands above his head to my headboard. He looks at his hands, then smiles at me.

"I think I love where this is going," Kody says, his voice dropping to a lustful level.

I kiss him long and hard, tangling my tongue with his we rub against each other. His naked cock against the zipper of my black slacks makes me second guess this entire going slow and worshiping my boy thing.

When I finally pull away, we're both gasping for breath. I run my fingers through his hair. "First, you're gonna suck my dick while I give yours the same treatment."

"Gladly." He thrusts into me.

I groan. "Such a bad boy." I press down against him, making him moan and hiss. "What are we gonna do about this?"

"Oh my God, don't stop," he breathes.

I do the exact opposite of his request and what I want to do. I pull myself off him. He tries to wrap his legs around me to get me to stay, but I'm too quick for that. I move to my knees at his side and grin when he whimpers at me.

"I'll make it worth the wait," I rumble as I unbutton the top three buttons of my white, button down shirt. I'm not patient enough to undo them all, so I pull it over my head and make quick work of my pants and underwear. I need my dick in his hot mouth.

Now.

I turn so I'm facing his feet before straddling his face. I grin at the moan as I position myself so my cock is lined up with his mouth. I lean forward and take his length in my mouth as I lower myself enough so he's sucking my dick comfortably without being smothered.

"Daddy, holy fuck," he mumbles around me.

I move my hips up and down so I'm fucking his mouth. The gagging sounds he makes when I slide down his throat and back out, make me regret everything about wanting to edge him. I want to taste him when he comes. I want him to swallow everything I give him.

Within seconds, we have a good rhythm set by me. The faster I thrust, the faster I suck him. He tries to arch into my mouth, but I hold his hips down. I want the control; need it. And he thrives off giving it to me; submitting to me.

I grip his thick, seven inch cock in my hand and start pumping it while I suck his tip. He screams around my length, and that's the end of it for me. I'm about to come. His stomach clenches tight. His thighs tremble.

I pull off him with an audible pop as I pull my own length out of his mouth. He's panting and writhing as he watches me. Words are on the tip of his mouth, but he's wise not to utter them. He knows I'll fuck him until he sees stars.

He just needs to be a patient boy.

My boy.

Chapter Ten

☾ Kody ☾

Hunter unties my hands. Before I can wrap myself around and push him to the bed, he's already on his back with me straddling him and positioned over his cock.

"Can't wait anymore. Ride me, baby."

My eyes widen when he slowly pushes me down onto his length. He's perfect. I grip his abs and close my eyes as he sinks into me deeper and deeper. It's not just the length and width of his dick that drives me insane. Hunter is very well built. He takes care of himself.

But the single that drives me so crazy for him is his incredible ability to sense exactly how I need him. Even if he's satiating his own needs, mine never go unnoticed or unsatisfied.

Just like now. He knows I need to feel him. All of him. Every ridge, muscle; every inch of him. He knows I need it slow and deliberate. He knows I need his hands on my body. He knows I need to focus all of my attention solely on him.

I know he needs me to ride him, but he'll give me everything I need first because it's who he is. Even if I start bouncing up and down and giving him everything he wants right now, he'll force me to back off so he can give me all that I do.

"You feel so good, my boy. So, so fucking good," Hunter squeezes his eyes closed once he's buried himself balls deep inside me.

I clench around him, making him gasp. He opens his eyes just as I start moving back and forth over him. Slowly. I keep him deep, not moving up and down. I love the way he feels moving back and forth inside me.

"Oh, daddy," I whisper. I love watching him. His eyes follow his hands as they roam over my body. "Please keep touching me." My eyes are hooded with lust.

"Gladly." He moves his hands up and down my legs to my ass. He moves up and down my back and to my chest. He moves lower down my stomach and across the base of my dick, but he never touches my length.

I'm so hard for him, and as his hands slowly explore the muscles of my body, my length remains fully erect and hard as diamonds. When I start to bounce, my cock does, too. I feel the precome beading from my tip, but actually watching it is fascinating. Especially when Hunter slides his thumb over it and sucks it into his mouth.

"So hot." The words fall from my lips like honey just waiting to be eaten up.

Hunter slowly moves his hands up my ass, his thumb still wet from sucking me off of it. He grips it and spreads my cheeks. We both growl at the change of sensations. He quickens the pace and starts thrusting into me while pushing down on his cock.

"Such a good boy for me. Look how good you take me, baby."

I turn my head. I'm not an owl so I can't see the best, but I see enough to know his dick looks incredible pumping in and out of my hole. I love the sound our skin makes slapping against each other. It turns me on even more.

When I turn and meet his sexy eyes once more, they've turned nearly red with fire. I don't know if that's the reflection for the sheets underneath us or if he really just became demonic for me, but I fucking love it.

Gradually, Hunter picks up speed. He starts slamming into me hard, deep, and fast enough for my dick to look like it's waving around. I'm so lost in how good he feels pounding me that I barely notice he's gripping my dick and stroking me like his life depends on it.

Or maybe it's my life that depends on him getting me off.

"Oh... my... fff... I can't..." I can't get the words out. I'm gonna come.

I clench hard around him and squeeze my eyes shut. If I come before he tells me to, he'll edge me all fucking night. It's fun, and he always lets me come, but not before my balls are blue. I can't deny the orgasm is the most powerful of all I've ever had, though.

But I don't want to be edged. I need to come. I need him to let me. I need to show him he's just as much mine as I am his, and I can't think of a better way to do that than to paint his chest with my come just like he's done to me so many times. My face, my ass, my dick, my stomach; my chest. I need to do it to him more than I need air.

"Almost, baby. Almost there, my boy." Hunter thrusts a few more times. He hits every spot I never knew I needed him to hit, and he does with zero effort. "Open your eyes. I want to see you when you come for me. Be my good boy, and I'll fill your ass up."

My eyes fly open. Hunter doesn't stop thrusting into me or jerking me, and when my orgasm hits, it hits hard. "Ah! Daddy!" I shout.

If anyone is near us, I'm sure they'll be calling the cops right now. I scream out like I'm being murdered. My come launches out of me like a fucking rocket. My entire body spasms with each jet of my spunk shooting out of me. The warm, white liquid hits Hunter on his stomach, chest, and face. He licks his lips as he slows his strokes and buries himself deep inside me.

"Oh fuck, Kody!" Hunter screams. My name on his lips as he fills my ass like he promised makes me come a second time. Hunter expertly guides me so I hit his chest and stomach as he jerks into me.

It takes several moments of deep, panting breaths before his semi-soft cock drops from my ass. I feel his come leaking from me as I fall to his side.

After a few more moments of silence, Hunter puts an arm around me and pulls me closer. "Heard anything about Riley?"

I sigh and nod as I lace our fingers. "Yeah. She's okay. Sterling is keeping an eye on her. I know he had to go out today without her, though. He didn't like that idea. He had a bike meet he's been looking forward to. He was gonna take her as his backpack, but Jacob wouldn't allow it."

"What the hell's a backpack? He shoves her in a backpack and carries her around?"

I laugh. "No. Not that. She rides on the back of his bike with him. Like his backpack. And if he needs anything, like his wallet, water, extra gear, or whatever she would need, that goes in a backpack that she would wear. So, she's his backpack and sometimes has her own backpack. The point was to keep her with him. He almost didn't go."

"I'm surprised he did."

"He texted when we were on the way home that she convinced him to, but that he wasn't staying long."

"What about Blade? Does he have guys he can put on her?"

"He has guys on her, but Jacob made it hard. He put security on her."

"Why does that set me uneasy?"

I take a deep breath. "Because of what Colt said when we talked to him. There's a lot of new people in town wearing suits and being intimidating. Like security."

We both fall silent. After a few moments, Hunter breaks it. "Seems to me more like henchmen."

I nod. "That's the way it feels to me, too. I think it feels that way to everyone."

"Well, may-" He's cut off by the ringing of my phone.

I reach over and pick it up. "It's Sterling," I say to Hunter as I answer. "Hey, man. We were just ta-"

"She's gone."

I sit up quickly. "What?"

"Riley. She's gone."

Something in his tone has me jumping up and throwing clothes on. "We'll be right there," I say as I hang up.

"What's going on?" Hunter asks. He's on his way to the bathroom to clean my come off himself, but I love how he's ready and willing to leave with me right now to be with my family.

"Riley's gone," I say.

"Fuck."

In a whirlwind, we both hurry to get dressed and run out to Hunter's truck. He peels out of the parking lot. If Sterling says Riley's gone, I believe him, and I don't doubt we'll find her.

What I fear is just how much he'll destroy to get to her.

The End

Concluding The Forbidden Temptation Series

The Forbidden Temptation Series concludes with *The Tight End's Forbidden Temptation*.

Riley. I could lose myself in the endless depths of her green eyes. She's intelligent, fun to talk to, and hang out with. I love getting to know things about her. I love even more that she challenges me. She's unlike any girl I've ever met.

And she's my stepsister.

Riley and I hit it off right away. Our parents got married not long after meeting. Things happened quickly. After they were married, I found out why.

We have a family secret. A big one. One that not even my cousins know.

But that's not even our biggest worry. Riley is being targeted, and we don't know who's behind the sinister plan to ruin her life.

Everyone has always thought Xavier was the most protective out of all of us. I've always been the quiet one standing behind everyone.

Ever wonder why an Alpha wolf stays at the end of his pack when they're traveling or hunting? It's because he's watching for threats. And he'll do anything to protect those he loves.

Everyone is about to find out who the Alpha of our group really is. Anyone who touches what's mine will face a wrath unlike anything they've ever faced.

Riley's mine.

Order your copy of *The Tight End's Forbidden Temptation* today!

The Forbidden Temptation Series

Available Now

The Detective's Forbidden Temptation
The Running Back's Forbidden Temptation
The Prez's Forbidden Temptation

Other Books By Melony Ann
The Beautiful Dream Series

Available Now

Loving You
My Love, My Heart
Softening Lyric
Undercover Temptations
Captain Charming
Breaking Boundaries
Crashing Into You
Tactical Inferno
Ravishing Our Queen
Cherished By The Texan
Unveiling Our Passions

Box Sets Available

The Beautiful Dream Series: Box Set: Part 1
The Beautiful Dream Series: Box Set: Part 2

The Crane Family Series

Available Now

The Reluctant Mafia King
Sweet Lies
Billion Dollar Love Story
Be Mine
Protecting Her
Dangerously Forbidden Love
His Heart
Love In The Dark

Box Sets Available

The Crane Family Series

The Deimos Trilogy

Available Now

Connor's Legacy
Aryan's Alpha
Kade's Redemption

Box Sets Available

The Deimos Trilogy

The Lucinio Family Series

Available Now

Rising From The Ashes
The Player's Rebel
Encrypting My Heart
Fighting My Fate
Phoenix Rising
Defending Her Honor

Multi Author Series
Piper Falls: Firehouse 49

Available Now

Ignite My Fire by Melony Ann
Regain My Fire by Kindra White
Playing With My Fire by D.L. Howe
Fight My Fire by Darley Collins
Against My Fire by Anneke Boshoff
Relight My Fire by Louise Murchie
Harness My Fire by Ayana Lisbet
Quench My Fire by Havana Wilder

Piper Falls: Station 28 Series

Available Now

Embracing My Duty by Melony Ann
Torn By My Duty by Kayla Baker
Against My Duty by Anneke Boshoff
Defying My Duty by D.L. Howe
Leave Of My Duty by Nikki A. Lamers
Fulfilling My Duty by Havana Wilder
Following My Duty by Louise Murchie
Replete In My Duty by Stacy Kristen
Accepting My Duty by Darley Collins

Let's Be Friends

Follow me on

Bookbub

Facebook

Goodreads

Instagram

Tik Tok

Visit my website
www.melonyannauthor.com

Subscribe to my newsletter and get a FREE never-seen-before NOVELLA
just for subscribers!
https://www.melonyannauthor.com/exclusive-ccntent

Join my Facebook Reader Group!
Melony Ann's Sizzling Book Nook

The official Forbidden Temptation Series Playlist on YouTube
https://youtube.com/playlist?list=PLGEiD5wbQmDfSjcIbdaBUl79mqR6t
URPP

Dedication

To everyone in a forbidden relationship. Follow your heart. Not the voices chirping at you.

Acknowledgements

To my loves.

To my friends.

To my team.

To the Bookstagram Community.

To my family.

To all of those who believe in me and support me.

To all of those who don't.

Cover by: Carter Cover Designs

Edited by: Alyssa Skaggs

About Melony Ann

Melony Ann began writing short stories and poetry as a child. She continued honing her craft over the years until she took the plunge and began publishing her work, despite having severe anxiety.

Melony writes contemporary romance stories that are full of suspense and a lot of steam.

When she isn't writing, she is loving her family and working to make her life something she deserves.

Melony believes that if her writing can inspire just one person, then all of her hard work is worth it.

Her hope is that her writing allows each and every one of her readers to escape for a little while. To dive into a different world one book at a time.